T0128547

Most titles are available online at web sites such as Barnes&Noble, Amazon, etc.

MAYAGUEZ AND THE MURDER SHIP:

TWO TALES OF MARITIME HEROISM

ROY F. SULLIVAN

authorHOUSE®

AuthorHouse™
1663 Liberty Drive
Bloomington, IN 47403
www.authorhouse.com
Phone: 1 (800) 839-8640

Published by AuthorHouse   05/22/2020

ISBN: 978-1-7283-6259-5 (sc)
ISBN: 978-1-7283-6258-8 (e)

Print information available on the last page.

IN GRATEFUL MEMORY OF THE BRAVE U.S.
MILITARY PERSONNEL WHO LOST THEIR LIVES
DURING THE JOINT MISSION TO
RECOVER THE CAPTURED CREW AND
THEIR VESSEL, THE S.S. MAYAGUEZ
12-15 MAY 1975
CAMBODIA (KAMPUCHEA)

Two US Navy Corpsmen
Seven US Air Force Crewmen
Fourteen US Marines
Eighteen US Air Force Security Police

Source: Wikipedia, "Mayaguez Incident"

FOR NANCY: EDITOR, CRITIC,
CO-CONSPIRATOR

CONTENTS

MEET THE CHARACTERS IN
ORDER OF APPEARANCE:

From the Peninsula Hotel, Hong Kong:

Captain Riley, master of the freighter *Sea Rover*, bon vivant

Captain Brownlee, master of the freighter *Malay Explorer*, part-time novelist

Mr. Thayer, chief engineer of the *Sea Rover*, formerly on the *Mayaguez* where he knew and admired First Mate Casey Flynn

On the Container Ship *Mayaguez*:

Captain Miles, calm, capable master of the *Mayaguez*

First Mate Casey Flynn, displayed heroism during the capture/release of the *Mayaguez*

Sa Mean, unpredictable Cambodian communist (Khmer Rogue) officer who seized their ship

MEET THE CREW OF THE OIL TANKER
"MURDER SHIP" (BANGOR) IN
ORDER OF APPEARANCE

Captain Casey Flynn, ambitious young master of his first ship, the *Bangor*

First Mate Avery, old experienced sea hand

Karl Friauf, Chief Engineer, proud of his reliable old diesels

Kathlee Sigmund, new Security Officer aspiring to become CEO of her father's shipping company

"Conejo" Tejada, Second Mate, normally on bridge watch

Seaman Saldana, nervous, newly-recruited seaman

Seaman Creech, mysteriously lost while on deck watch at night

Seaman Cruz, newly recruited with Saldana, often working in engine room

"Papa" Alonzo, Cook, busy preparing large meals for a diminishing crew

"Smitty" Smithson, helmsman, poor sleeper suffering frequent nightmares

"Pancho" Partagas, seaman, often on night deck patrol

Franz Suppe, Second Engineer, curious about topside happenings

PROLOGUE

THE WATERS OFF Kowloon at seven a.m. were unusually murky and choppy due to festering disturbances remaining from tropical depression Carlos. Nonetheless the channel was filled with freighters and cargo carriers emptily bobbing at anchor, having earlier unloaded their cargoes at the seaport.

Far above the channel two grey-bearded men slouched in deck chairs, alternately sipping mai tais and flipping peanut hulls over the edge of the wide veranda of Hong Kong's famous old Peninsula Hotel.

"How was your evening?" One asked, winking at the other, sure of the answer.

They both reveled in the formality of their titles although they knew each other very well after years of sea service.

"You saw us in the elevator, Captain?"

"Yes, Captain, I certainly did," the questioner grinned. "She was lovely! And so young! Surprised you were able to make it down to breakfast this morning!"

Raising his empty glass, Captain Riley signaled the waiter for more drinks. "I attribute my stamina in the sack to plenty of sea air and cold showers aboard my modest vessel, *Sea Rover.*"

Riley countered by eyeing his friend in amusement. "Bet you went to bed by yourself. Still dallying with your memoirs or sea stories...or whatever? Must keep you up all hours."

"I did, that is--go to bed by myself--and yes, I still dabble at writing the Great American Sea Story." Captain Brownlee answered, downing the last of his drink.

"You see," Brownlee wiped his chin, reflecting. "I strive to set a good example for the impressionable young crew of my *Malay Explorer.*"

Riley smirked, acknowledging the new drink handed him by the waiter.

Despite their chiding, the two captains toasted each other with the new drinks. "Bottoms up!"

Riley lifted the binoculars hanging from his neck and leaned forward, studying his freighter in the distant waters below.

"Afraid they'll get under way without you?" Brownlee joked.

"Wrong, Captain! The first mate is blowing out the funnels today, just as I instructed when I came ashore yesterday. Gross is a damned good first mate, the best in the entire *Seatrans* fleet, I wager!"

Brownlee groused. "Obviously, you haven't heard the exploits of First Mate Casey Flynn of the *Mayaguez.*"

"Yeah, I've heard lots of stories about 'Famous Flynn' and the *Mayaguez* capture but I think it's all a crock. It's just a collection of hearsay intended to impress the youngsters coming out of the maritime academy!"

Tired of each other's morning-long banter about ships and crews, their conversation faltered. Exasperated, the two eyed each other. Neither wanted to return to his ship and forego the pleasures of Hong Kong any earlier than necessary.

After hours of comparing ships' speed, power plants, crew problems, next ports and retirement plans, what was left?

Finally, Riley lit a cigar and studied Brownlee through the pungent smoke. "What say we later meet at the main bar and see what's going down there? Might be some lovelies there looking for a couple of viral young sea captains."

Sitting upright, Brownlee studied his new Japanese watch, before agreeing. "Flank speed! See you there in six bells!"

The two captains, surrounded by several fetching ladies, sat at the Peninsula's famous, gilded main bar exactly three hours later. A small combo in the nearby lounge began blaring so loudly that the two left their female companions at the bar and retreated to a far table.

"No more of those fancy concoctions," Riley proposed, pounding the table "We need whiskey! Right?"

Brownlee dutifully agreed by striking the table even harder, causing a waiter to rush to their table.

"Bring us a bottle of good Scotch, ice and two big tumblers. We'll make this next-to- last-night in port a memorable one!"

Another man, dressed in navy blue, now stood at the bar, taking the captains' former chairs, and ordering himself a drink.

"Hey!" Riley pointed. "There's my Chief Engineer! Mind if I ask him over?"

Brownlee looked up from pouring two tumblers half-full. "Course not. He's probably looking for you to help bail your crew out of a Hong Kong jail."

"Mister Thayer!" Riley called, waving his hand. "C'mon over! Join us for a drink."

"Captain Brownlee, this is my Chief Engineer, Mr. Thayer. Mr. Thayer, shake hands with Captain Brownlee, master of the *Malay Explorer.*"

"A pleasure, sir," Thayer responded smoothly, reluctantly switching his gaze from the avid ladies lining the bar.

"We were just talking about the famous First Mate of the *Mayaguez.*

"Captain Brownlee here is a man who was aboard the *Mayaguez* with First Mate Flynn. The two of you probably have a lot to talk about.

"But watch him, Mr. Thayer. Captain Brownlee may put your name in one of his novels and make you famous--or infamous--throughout the fleet."

A third tumbler and more ice appeared on the table. After several more drinks, the two captains seemed to unwind in the presence of the bearded engineer, busily detailing the conditions of his section's new diesels.

"How's our crew doing, Mr. Thayer? Many absentees among the crew in this flesh- pot port?"

Rather than facing his engineer for an answer, Riley was looking over the other's shoulder at a lady beckoning him from the bar.

"Just the usual, Captain," Thayer answered. "A few hands returned to the ship a bit under the weather. No arrests, fights or bloodshed so far."

As the conversation continued about past incidents with their crews, Riley's attention focused on the beckoning female at the bar. Eventually, he put down his cigar and made the point of looking at his watch.

"Afraid it's the bewitching hour for me, gentlemen. If you'll excuse me, I'm off to the room to practice using my sextant."

Brownlee and Thayer watched Riley stand, then pause. He asked. "Mind if I take the remainder of this Scotch to my room?"

"Have at it, Captain," Brownlee gestured. "Think I'll switch to wine with dinner. Please join me, Mr. Thayer."

They watched Captain Riley walk away, nodding at the girl at the bar to follow him.

Embarrassed, Brownlee cleared his throat and turned to Thayer. "I'd like to hear all about your experiences with First Mate Flynn and the *Mayaguez*.

"Seldom do I have such an opportunity to hear about them from an actual witness to that famous incident. I invite you to dine with me, at the expense of my million questions and note-taking." Brownlee produced a pen and small notebook as if to illustrate his threat.

Thayer arose and they walked out of the bar into the next door dining room. "I'm always pleased to talk about my old friend, Casey Flynn, and his exploits."

Thayer took the seat across from Brownlee. "Too little is known about Casey whom I consider to be a modern day marine hero. I'd be pleased to relate what I know firsthand or have heard about him, but dinner isn't necessary, Captain."

"Oh, I insist, Mr. Thayer."

"Thank you, Captain. I'll accept if you'll call me James since we're off duty."

Table cleared, wine finished, cigars and brandy at hand, Captain Brownlee opened his notebook and looked expectantly at the engineer. At this, Thayer nodded and began speaking.

"I'm uncertain what you have heard in the past or read somewhere, so I'll start with the ship. Captain Charles Miles was master, Casey Flynn, our first mate, and I was the engineering officer. Our crew numbered thirty nine men.

"It was a large crew since the *Mayaguez* itself was almost 430 feet long, 63 feet broad, 40 feet deep and with a 25 foot draft.

"We were bound for Sattahip, Thailand, from Hong Kong with the usual load of petroleum products, seventy-seven containers of government and military equipment plus almost 100 empty containers. The date was May 12, a date I'm not likely to forget.

"We'd drawn Sattahip as our destination before, so often, our headings were familiar. So we considered this an easy passage, without incident.

"We knew of the recent revolution of same sort in Cambodia on our way to Thailand. Certainly we'd received no maritime warnings about territorial water claims or disputes or what the Cambodian navy might do to enforce such claims.

"You may wonder how I recall dates and hours so precisely: It's because I've narrated these events often, but with little effect upon my listeners. I hope from your professed interest and note-taking that you might do something--write, even publish something--which recognizes Casey's heroism. I'd be highly appreciative if you would do so. His story--I think it a maritime legacy--begs to be heard."

Brownlee put out his cigar. "James, you inspire me to attempt just that. I'll try not to burden you with questions until you are through. Meanwhile, here's a new bottle of Scotch. Let's sample it!"

Thayer chuckled. "Then we may be here for several hours, Captain. Well… here goes.

"It was on the afternoon of May 12, at 1418 hours, when a small armed vessel flying a Cambodian flag (we presumed it was their navy) approached from the mainland, firing a machinegun across our bow! Captain Miles immediately ordered me to slow to maneuver speed.

"Even below in the engine room I heard the rapid firing. All of us below were paralyzed by the ratta-tat-tat. Captain Miles issued us a terse order and we slacked speed, still not knowing the situation topside.

"The next sound we heard in the engine room was an explosion, a large POW! Moments later, we were told by the bridge that the Cambodians had fired a rocket propelled grenade across our bow which exploded loudly when it hit the water.

"I credit Captain Miles and First Mate Flynn for their calm reactions during this attack. There must have been pandemonium on the bridge.

"The captain dispatched an SOS and ordered me to stop the turbines.

"We were dead in the water and the Cambodian vessel, later described as a Swift Boat, bumped alongside and seven armed Cambodian soldiers and an officer boarded us. They captured and rounded-up us, the very frightened crew of the *Mayaguez.*

"Unknown to us at the time, these Cambodians were the communist victors, known as the Khmer Rouge, of their recent revolution in Cambodia, now called Kampuchea.

"Shouting and pointing their AK-47 rifles at us, the soldiers assembled the entire crew on the main deck. For a few minutes I thought they were going to shoot us and toss our bodies overboard.

"Once things calmed down a few degrees, their officer pointed on his map where we should proceed once we revived the turbines. The area the officer pointed to was east of a small nearby island called Poulo Wai.

"Our position when we were captured was two nautical miles south of Poulo Wai. We were not flying our usual flag as loudly pointed out by the Cambodian officer named Sa Mean, rank unknown, continually waving his pistol.

"Luckily, during the ruckus, one member of our crew was able to send a Mayday message which was monitored by a nearby Australian vessel. Thank God the Australians relayed the Mayday to their authorities, who notified the U.S. Embassy. Our records never identified the crew member who succeeded in sending that Mayday. I'm certain it was Casey Flynn."

Thayer refilled his glass and added more ice. "You can bet I'll ask him the next time I see him.

"Back to my timeline. At 1600 hours we had reached the area the Khmer Rouge officer indicated. Another twenty soldiers, also brandishing AK47s, gleefully boarded us from another Swift Boat.

"This time Sa Mean, the officer pointing his cocked pistol at everyone, told Captain Miles that we were to proceed north to the Ream Naval Base, formerly home of the Royal Cambodian Navy.

"Luckily, Captain Miles and Casey Flynn came through again. They were successful in convincing Sa Mean that our radar was not working and without it the *Mayaguez* would end up on the hidden coastal reefs, perhaps even sink.

"I'll never forget Casey's pantomime to illustrate what might happen if we proceeded inland without radar. He was so effective that Sa Mean radioed Casey's warning to his superiors somewhere and we were allowed to remain at Poulo Wai."

Thayer put a hand on his forehead, as if refreshing his memory. "So we dropped anchor off Poulo Wai at 1655 hours, almost an hour after we had been boarded.

"We spent that night, trying to sleep on the bare main deck under the scrutiny of the Khmer Rouge soldiers, posted all around us. It was not a restful night.

"Believe me, there were plenty of prayers emanating from that deck that night! We had no idea if either the Captain's SOS or the later Mayday message--which I still think Casey somehow managed to transmit--had been received, believed or acted upon.

"The next morning, cookie was allowed to bring us lukewarm coffee from the galley. It was the best coffee I've ever tasted and tended to lighten our spirits. The date was March 13. We received even better news than the coffee in a few minutes.

"Two US Navy aircraft, someone later identified as Orions, made several passes at us and dropped flares. Standing on deck, we all waved and shouted as loudly as we could until the soldiers began pointing their AKs at us and firing at the Orions. The planes flew away to the east.

"At least one of our attempts to tell the world about our capture had been received and Uncle Sam was on the way! We hoped!"

Thayer took a long drink and toasted their imaginary

uncle. "May seem silly to you," he cackled, "but it was dead serious to us, shivering on that wet deck after a sleepless night. We were **elated** that we'd been found! I'd never understood that word so well!"

Brownlee chuckled as he refilled both tumblers. "Bravo!"

"Back to the ship," Thayer resumed. "A few minutes after the two Orions departed, another took their place, also dropping flares and again drawing fire from the Khmer Rouge soldiers. The time, by my wrist watch, was 0815 hours.

"The aerial parade resumed again while we were issued a half bowl of rice on the deck by our ship's cook. This time (1300 hours) it was two USAF F-111 fighter bombers overhead. The frightened soldiers again blazed away with their ineffective rifles, littering the desk with spent brass. An excited Sa Mean also reacted, ordering us to immediately get underway and follow two Swift Boats to a small island marked "Koh Tang" on our charts.

"We dropped anchor about 1.5 kilometers north of the new island, Koh Tang."

At this, Thayer clapped his hands. "More aerial company appeared, this time two USAF F4 Phantom jets who made us all sweat a bit by firing their 20mm cannon ahead and behind the stern of the *Mayaquez*, plainly indicating the ship should not move.

"To emphasize the point to an already highly agitated Sa Mean, two more F4s, more F-111s, and two A-7D Corsairs arrived and repeated their 'don't you dare move' lesson. It was more airpower than the awed communists--us included-- had ever seen.

"Sa Mean was apoplectic, continually radioing his higher headquarters, wherever that was. He kept waving his arms and screaming at his men to shoot down the jets with their AKs and machineguns. Even their machineguns, which Casey somehow identified as 7.62 mm Type 56s, posed no danger to our fast aircraft.

Thayer cleared his memory again and smiled. "Now it was 1615 hours and we were ordered off our ship and onto two fishing boats. Sa Mean was acting so erratically that neither Captain Miles nor Casey questioned him more than once about our destination.

"In any case, we were highly worried about our safety. Behind us, we watched our lovely *Mayaguez* recede from sight. The smelly fishing boats, so heavily laden with us they almost swamped, headed east toward the island of Koh Tang. We hoped," Thayer breathed deeply, "Koh Tang wasn't to be our private cemetery.

"Once there, the soldiers crowded us into a small, barbed-wire enclosure on the island, where we spend the night amid a million sand crabs. The soldiers offered us another half-bowl of cold, cooked rice. Oddly enough, the rice seemed to raise our spirits, despite the surly attitude of our captors, who rattled the barbed-wire separating us from them with their bayonets all night.

"It was now May14, our third day of increasing apprehension. Some of the crew thought we'd be taken to the Cambodian capital, Phnom Penh, for a public show trial. Others said the 82d Airborne Division probably was enroute from the U.S. and would be dropped over Koh Tang to free us once it was dark.

"The Captain, particularly First Mate Casey Flynn, walked around, talking to everyone, trying to raise morale and allay fears. Casey allowed we were 'too expensive' for the Khmer Rouge to keep. 'We eat too much," he quipped.

At their hotel dining room, Brownlee and Thayer chuckled. At this break in Thayer's story, Brownlee raised a hand.

"Mind if I smoke?"

"Not at all," Thayer responded. "I'll join you by lighting my old pipe."

"Fine," Brownlee grinned as he uttered the familiar naval phrase, 'The smoking lamp is lit.'

Quickly, he followed with "May I pour you another splash of Scotch?"

The two men toasted each other with raised tumblers. "Is this too fast for you to take notes?" Thayer asked, after a deep draught from his glass.

"Fine, so far. I find your recollection very valuable as well as entertaining. I'm already imagining a major book which will knock the socks off both my editor and publisher."

"Then back to my time line," Thayer tried to relight his pipe without success, then put it aside.

"That morning, May 14, we were marched by the soldiers from our barbed-wire corral on the beach onto the larger of the two fishing boats that brought us to Koh Tang. Captain Miles and First Mate Flynn pantomimed to Sa Mean 'Where are we going?'

Sa Mean pointed to his small map and indicated our destination was Kompong Som. A coastal town, it was just over the hill from the Ream Naval Base. That's where Sa Mean said we were going before Casey Flynn convinced him of the hazard of moving the *Mayaguez* without radar.

"This time our smelly fishing boat was preceded by two Cambodian Swift Boats. Seconds later someone shouted and pointed up. We were thrilled and roared approval of a sky-full of U.S. aircraft. Two F-11s swept by our fishing boat, followed by two F-4 Phantoms, Another pair, A-7D Corsairs, screamed into view. The last four aircraft began firing into the water in front of the Swift Boats, then shifted their fire **at** them. One of the Swift Boats made a sharp turn and headed toward Koh Tang.

"To our surprise, a big C-130 Spectre gunship next arrived,

joining the fray, and firing at the remaining Swift Boat. One of the A-7Ds sank that Swift Boat with its 20mm cannon."

Thayer took a deep breath and looked to see if Brownlee was keeping up.

"You can't imagine the scene! There were so many of our planes up there and they were there to safeguard us if at all possible. A grand feeling!

"To prove it, the fighters began firing ahead of our fishing boat and dropping bombs nearby. They flew so close, they could count us. We later found they had radioed there were 30 to 40 of us aboard that fishing boat. Damned accurate count from a thousand feet up!

"By 1010 hours, our fishing boat reached Kompong Som to the northeast, on the coast. The local Khmer Rouge commander, fearing he would be the next target of our aircraft, refused to let our fishing boat stop. He was prescient. One of his patrol boats was sinking and four more ablaze a short distance away.

"So this commander refused to let our fishing boat remain. Leaking and overloaded, we were forced to move west to another island, This one was labeled Koh Rong Sanloem on Sa Mean's map.

"Once ashore at the new island, Koh Rong Sanloem, the Captain and First Mate were interrogated by another Khmer Rouge commander. Casey later told us this officer wanted to know if we could communicate with our U.S. aircraft. He snarled that he had already lost three boats and many casualties since our capture.

"Miles and Casey explained they could communicate only if they were back on the *Mayaguez* and generating electricity to call our commercial office in Bangkok. That office would then relay any message to the U.S. military.

"The communist commander relayed our conversation

to his higher headquarters. Eventual permission was given to return the Captain, First Mate Flynn and nine men to our ship to establish communications with Bangkok. Since it was already dark, permission was withheld until daylight on the next day, May 15."

"Whew, if darkness was the reason for their delay, I suggest we retire since it's also dark here…almost midnight." Captain Brownlee held up both hands in the hotel dining room.

"Let's resume your extremely interesting review in the morning after a good breakfast," he suggested.

Thayer nodded agreement and closed his folder of notes. "I apologize for talking so long, Captain. I'll condense the remainder tomorrow."

"No, no, no," Brownlee exclaimed as he stood. "Please don't condense anything! Your memory is as remarkable as this important event. I desperately want it all!"

Brownlee studied the engineer officer. "I suggest we meet for breakfast here in this room at 0900 tomorrow and resume this fascinating subject."

Thayer gathered his papers. "I'd be delighted to meet you at 0900, Captain. But I insist on buying our breakfast."

With that, the two left the room.

Brownlee was the first to speak the next morning. "Before sacking-out this morning, I reviewed my hasty notes. They are the basis of a stirring story I'm anxious to start writing once aboard my ship."

Thayer was trying to light his pipe. "I'm pleased you think it useful. Today I'm covering the busy events of the morning of May 15.

"It began at 0607 hours when a Khmer Rouge minister in Phnom Penh made a radio announcement that our ship and crew would be released!

"I later found a translation of his broadcast and here's a copy for your notes:

> Regarding the *Mayaguez* ship. We have no intention of detaining it permanently and we have no desire to stage provocations. We only wanted to know the reason for its coming and to warn it against violating our waters again. That is why our coast guard seized this ship. Their goal was to examine it, question it and make a report to higher authorities who would then report to the Royal Government so that the Royal Government could itself decide to order it to withdraw from Cambodia's territorial waters and warn it against conducting further espionage and protractile activities.

"A few minutes later, at 0630 hours on Koh Rong Sanloem Island, we were told we could return to the *Mayaguez* if we would sign statements that we had not been mistreated. If you can imagine our glee, we signed those statements faster than a ship's monthly payroll!

"But there were, of course, more hurdles. We were loaded onto another fishing boat, escorted by a second boat containing Sa Mean and his soldiers. We were instructed to return to the *Mayaguez* and 'call-off those American airplanes.'

"At 0949 our fishing boat was intercepted by the destroyer *USS Wilson* and we happily--no, deliriously--climbed aboard the *Wilson*.

"Earlier, at 0612 hours, U.S. forces began rescue operations on Koh Tang, not realizing that we of the *Mayaguez* were elsewhere. At the time, we were on Koh Rong Sanloem and being released by the Khmer Rouge."

Thayer breathed heavily and dabbed his eyes with the breakfast napkin. "That ends my notes and recollections of that terrible event. Terrible, since we of the *Mayaguez* cannot forget the sacrifices made by our military to rescue us from the Khmer Rogue.

"Fifteen Americans were killed in action. Tragically, three more young men, Marines, were captured and murdered in a most gristly fashion by the Khmer Rouge. Twenty-three more Americans were killed attempting our helicopter rescue. Yet more Americans, fifty of them, were wounded during the rescue operation."

The two men sat without speaking at the breakfast table. Finally, Captain Brownlee looked up. "I guess you know where your friend, Casey Flynn, ended up?"

"Yes, Captain. I heard he was highly acclaimed by Captain Miles as well as the *Seatrans* president, Mr. Sigmund, for Casey's actions and bravery on the *Mayaguez*. He is even on the short list, being considered for a captain command despite his age. Sure hope he makes it!"

"Well, James, I'm the bearer of good news! Casey Flynn was promoted and offered the command of an old fuel tanker, the *Bangor*."

Thayer leaped out of his chair. "Hooray for Casey! Well deserved!"

Brownlee grinned. "But there's a bit more to the scuttlebutt I've heard from other captains. The *Bangor* is well-known as for its problems: accidents, old engines, crew discipline, so much so that a Security Officer is being added to Casey's normal crew."

"So...sounds reasonable," Thayer squinted in anticipation of the rest.

"The Security Officer assigned to Casey is the daughter of the *Seatrans* president! She's said to be a beautiful young lady! Her assignment to the *Bangor* is to give her operational experience, maybe eventually to replace her father when he retires!"

"Oh," Thayer's squint became a grimace. "Poor Casey! Saddled with an infamous ship, difficult crew and new Security Officer--a good-looking female!

"Bet he'll wish he were back on the good old *Mayaguez!*"

CHAPTER ONE

E ARLY MORNING IN Singapore's harbor is always a revelation. Overhead, terns and gulls circle, avidly searching the waters for their breakfast. The young officer striding purposefully down the pier could not pause to enjoy the sights and sounds of the scene.

Newly-commissioned Captain Casey Flynn had no time to admire the birds or the colored mists rising from the choppy tide. Instead he climbed the gangway of his first command, the small, rather nondescript coastal oil tanker, its stern marked *Bangor.*

Grimly he noticed the accumulated rust and barnacles of previous voyages as he climbed to the deck and acknowledged the half-salute of the First Mate waiting at the rail.

"Welcome aboard, Captain." Frowning, First Mate Avery offered him a gnarled hand, gesturing with the other.

"Right this way, sir. All hands are assembled in the mess. Our tanks are topped off, turbines warming, and we're ready to cast off at your pleasure, Captain."

Flynn smiled, as yet unused to his title. He was meeting his new crew, repeat the phrases practiced last night in front of his hotel room mirror and join them for lunch. He prepared himself for the surprise evident on their faces. Flynn was only thirty years old, by far the youngest captain in the *Seatrans* fleet.

"I'll show them all" he silently promised himself as he

entered the mess. "Competent and confident!" The crew scrambled to its feet as the First Mate cried 'Attention".

"Seats, please!" was his first instruction aboard this, his first vessel. He walked down both sides of the long mess table, looking each man in the eye, shaking hands and associating faces with the names memorized from the fleet roster mailed him. Then he faced them from the head of the table and repeated thirty minutes of traditional guidance to his new crew.

The handshaking and introductions in the mess allowed his officers to precede Flynn to the wardroom for another meeting. The cook poured coffee as Flynn and the two men took seats. There were only two officers, Flynn nodded, whom he'd just met in the mess.

Three men, including me, Flynn repeated to himself. On his left sat the Engineer Officer, Mr. Friauf. Next was Avery, the First Mate.

Friauf, the Engineer, raised a hand to speak.

"Captain, your Second Mate, Andres Tejada, is at the airport picking up your new--and I do mean new--female Security Officer Sigmund." Friauf started to chuckle but stopped at Flynn's frozen expression.

"Yes, I know of her assignment," Flynn nodded, stirring his coffee. "Despite her gender and lack of experience, I expect each of us to treat Security Officer Sigmund like we would any new officer. Is that understood?"

"Yes, sir!" Friauf and Avery assured him.

"Now, I'd like to hear your section reports. Afterwards, we'll inspect the ship together."

A half-mile away, two figures were descending the pier to sit in a lighter which would ferry them to the *Bangor*. The first was a young woman dressed sailor-style in dark sweater and practical work pants. Her auburn hair glinted beneath a woolen watch cap as she selected an empty seat. If the purpose of the sailor's garb was to disguise her feminine form, it failed. Sailors, even elderly passengers on the ferry, gaped.

Azure eyes glanced at the man beside her, wearing a *Seatrans* wind breaker. Second Mate Tejada met her at the airport, helped her through customs and immigration, then they took a bus to the pier.

"Thanks again for meeting me, Second Mate. Hope I wasn't the only reason you were in town?"

"No, ma'm," Tejada shook his head. "I was supposed to hire us a couple of replacements. But…no luck.

"Call me 'Conejo', ma'm, if you like. Everybody has a nickname on the *Bangor*."

He shook his head. "Signing on new hands sounds easy, I know, but it's not. I couldn't sign up a single man."

"Why is that, Conejo?"

Tejada shrugged muscular shoulders. "Dunno, but our new captain--and you, ma'm--will have your hands full keeping a full crew!"

"No, thanks," she shook her head to his offer of a cigarette. "Why is it hard to get replacements?"

Tejada flipped his cigarette butt overboard. "Some say our ship is spooked. I know it sounds silly but a replacement might jump ship at our next port…or just disappear!"

"Disappear? How is that possible?"

"Some are carried off sick, ma'm. Others are carried off to the morgue. Either way, they never come back."

Tejada scratched his head. "Maybe that's why you're coming to the *Bangor* to solve our mystery?

"God," Tejada moaned, pointing as the lighter approached their ship.

"Look what someone's painted on our bow!"

There, scrawled in white, was **MURDER SHIP.**

CHAPTER TWO

ONCE SHE CLAMBERED aboard the *Bangor's* steep ladder, followed by Tejada heisting her sea bag, she almost collided with her new captain.

"Security Officer Sigmund reports to Captain Flynn for duty, sir!" she snapped, eyes widening at the youth of her new boss.

"Welcome aboard, Sigmund. Glad to have you here!" Casey almost added softly, "in Spades!"

"Seaman Saldana, here, will show you to your cabin and help you stow your gear." Casey eyed her hefty sea bag.

He caught his breath, never having seen his new security officer before. "This is First Mate Avery, who will fetch you for supper in the mess in thirty minutes. After that, we'll have a short meeting and walk you about for a familiarization tour of your new home, the *Bangor*."

Sigmund blinked rapidly, absorbing his words as well as his startling blue eyes. "Aye, aye, sir," she managed, turning to catch up with the seaman carrying her bag down a narrow passageway.

Over her shoulder she heard Flynn speak to the First Mate, "Get that white paint or whatever it is removed from the bow! Any clue who painted it there?"

After a simple meal of stew, salad and hot biscuits, Captain

Flynn repeated his welcome to the Security Officer, already introduced to the Engineer and First Mate.

"Any idea who painted our bow?" Flynn again asked the First Mate. "Let's get that white painted 'MURDER SHIP' removed!"

"The bow's already clean, Captain," the First Mate reported. "As to who did it, had to be someone in maintenance. No one else has access to the paint locker."

Immediately, Friauf, the engineer, raised an objection. "Could have been anyone on board, Captain. Everyone knows where that locker is and that it's usually unlocked."

Flynn turned to Sigmund, sitting across from him. "Any suggestions, Security?"

"Yes, sir. Let's check the fingernails of everyone for traces of white paint."

First Mate Avery shook his head. "The culprit could have removed any white paint traces with gasoline hours ago."

"But not necessarily under all fingernails," Sigmund countered.

"Worth a try," Flynn decided, turning to the First Mate. "Please organize and conduct a search. Can you manage it before supper? Let me know the results this evening."

"Still plan on getting underway in the morning, Captain?"

"Yes, tides should be favorable by 0500 hours."

On her way out of the mess, Flynn halted her. "Please remain. We have a more pressing problem to discuss than white paint.

"You see, Security Officer, there really has been a murder on board!"

"Oh, no!" Reluctantly, she resumed the chair opposite his.

"I know," he watched her reaction. "Hell of a way to begin our new assignments! Here's what I was told by the First Mate when I arrived. Two nights ago, after refueling at the refinery depot, a sailor named Creech was on guard duty, walking the deck from midnight until 0600 that morning.

"It was dark and Creech was alone. No one admits to hearing anything during the night. The next morning there was no sign of Creech… anywhere."

"You searched the ship, Captain?"

"First Mate told me he supervised it personally. No Creech, no body."

By now, Sigmund was taking notes in her ever-present I-pad. "What kind of person was Creech? Stable? Could he have jumped ship and made it to shore somehow?"

"Excellent questions, Security Officer, and I have no answers. The First Mate reported Creech missing to the Singapore police but they've reported nothing."

"Does the crew know?" she asked.

"No," Flynn admitted. "Neither the First Mate nor I have announced his absence. I don't know my new crew but telling them might be unwise. They might all jump ship."

"But someone on board this vessel must know where Creech is," he stared at her pensively.

Sigmund agreed. "Whoever painted 'MURDER SHIP' on the bow knows Creech is gone, Captain. That mysterious painter may be responsible for Creech's death."

CHAPTER THREE

"**R**IGHT ON!" FLYNN banged the table. "And we've got to prevent anything like this happening again!"

"Starting tonight, when we're underway," she pursed her lips, "let's put **two** seamen on deck guard,. They'll also be checking on and reassuring each other."

Flynn leaned forward, touching her arm. "We can order the bridge to turn on the deck lights at different intervals to keep them alert. I'll be out there, too, at all hours."

"No, Captain. We'll share that duty. **I'm** the security officer. We can't afford to lose our captain."

Flynn laughed "We're both just assigned, have new responsibilities and already facing our first crisis--a huge one! Murder!"

"Possible murder, Captain," she moved her arm. "Possibly Creech was suicidal?"

"You're right, of course. No use panicking. But the crew is certain to realize something strange is going on. I'm fortunate having you aboard, investigating--as you call it---a possible murder.

"You see," he grinned, "I must prove to your father that he made the right choice in selecting me for command. I must make this ship the best in the whole damn fleet…and do it overnight."

"I'm here to assist you do just that, Captain."

With that, Flynn rang for the First Mate. "Let's take that tour of the ship I promised you."

"Do you always keep your promise, Captain?" she taunted.

Before he could reply, a grinning First Mate joined them for the tour. "Let's first go below, see the engines, pumps and storage tanks. They are the heart of our operation."

Avery led them down a steep companionway, opening and closing hatches while pointing and explaining each device or piece of equipment.

"A larger ship than I thought," she mused while accidentally bumping Captain Flynn in the companionway.

"She's fifty meters long and double-hulled," Flynn recited. "Her draft is four meters. Compared to those giants in your father's fleet, we're a peanut."

It was the First Mate's time to boast. "We may be old and slow but we are an **important** peanut. We are the ideal inter-island transport."

Avery stepped deeper into the dark interior of the ship. "If you are wondering about the noise and vibration down here, it's because our turbines are operating. They maintain our relative position while we're being loaded through hoses from a refinery."

Eager to exhibit knowledge of his new command, Flynn added, "We can carry up to nine hundred-fifty DWT, dead weight tons. You know the term?"

"Sure," Sigmund replied. Moving on, she pointed. "Bet those are Cummins K19 diesels, rated at 1800 RPM.

"Revolutions per minute," she added with a grin at Flynn. She pointed proudly to a control panel. "I've learned from my father how to operate diesels, generators and most of the other equipment down here."

"Bet you even know the *Bangor's* top speed," Flynn patted her shoulder.

"I do," she removed his hand. "Your new command is

capable of fifteen knots, depending on cargo and weather, of course."

Blushing, Flynn removed his hand. "Of course."

Grinning at his reaction, she added, "That's not bad considering she's twelve years old."

Recovering, he countered, "So you think age is a big factor?"

"It's certainly a deterrent," she turned away, pointing at the centrifugal pumping station straddling the entire quarter.

"To illustrate the size of our beam, those pumps occupy over twenty feet."

Flynn held up a hand, as if in a classroom. "How did you absorb all this so quickly?"

"Father taught me the basics on whatever ship was idle. He often said that the best place to learn the business is as a security officer on a small vessel."

She shrugged. "Father wanted a son, but here I am!"

"I'm admiring the future president of *Seatrans* Transports," Flynn shook her hand.

"Bet you loved that movie *Captain Phillips*."

She pointed a finger. "Don't tease the security officer, Captain."

Motioning them forward, First Mate Avery pointed to a huge steel tank preventing their passage. "That's tank number four, already loaded. Our maximum capacity is 800,000 barrels.

"Along the inside, lining the hull are ballast tanks being adjusted to maintain trim once we are underway. Let's go forward so you can see the immensity of the tanks and their total capacity," Avery gestured.

"Speaking of trim, there's our engineer officer, Karl Friauf, doing just that. We'll see him again upstairs when he's not concentrating on keeping us afloat as the other tanks are being loaded."

It was Flynn's turn to point. "Over there are our fuel

consumption monitors next to the combustion manifold, temperature gauges and voltage regulators."

Flynn pointed again. "Behind us are several systems to cool fresh water, generate potable water, even measure bilge and sludge.

"Speaking of that, Kathlee, how do you manage to smell like fresh flowers in the middle of all this grime and oil?"

Sigmund drew a deep breath at Flynn's use of her first name. The First Mate looked away, studying his watch.

"Time to go forward so you can get an idea of the immensity of the tanks and our total capacity. Maybe we'll catch a glimpse of another engineer, Franz Suppe, at work. Most of the crew is topside at the moment loading and rehearsing safety measures.

"Safety is paramount on an oil tanker." Avery added solemnly.

In thirty minutes, their walk-about finished, Flynn and Sigmund stood on the bridge.

"Is your cabin alright?" he asked.

"It's fine, Captain."

"I need to see you privately, preferably there, for a moment."

CHAPTER FOUR

NERVOUSLY, SHE FIDDLED a second with the key before her cabin door opened. "Is this an inspection, Captain?"

"No, ma'm," Flynn grinned. "I wanted to ask in private, what's your first impression of our ship?"

Wondering what else was on his mind, she gestured to a chair.

"Same as yours, Captain."

"Which is?"

"Since you asked my opinion, your ship needs a lot of work. You could have asked me that on the bridge."

"Forgive my intrusion in your cabin, but I also wanted to give you this." he handed her a small semiautomaic pistol, "in private. Ever fire a pistol?"

She studied the pistol placed in her hand. "Hmm, a Glock 9mm. My father taught me to shoot his Colt .45, so this will be easy.

"Thank you, Captain I'm impressed with your concern for your greenhorn security officer. Yes, before you say it, I will be careful with this weapon."

Flynn caught his breath as she looked up at him but murmured, "Please carry it concealed every time you are out of your cabin, especially at night."

He backed up a step. "By the way, you mentioned that age is a big factor. May I ask how old you are?"

"I'm twenty-two," she laughed. "Now who's concerned about age?"

He took another deep breath. "I apologize for using your first name a bit ago. I won't do that again, I assure you."

"Save me time, Captain Flynn. Tell me how you got here, the youngest captain in the fleet. Were you raised in the States?"

"Yes ma'm. In Georgia, near Fort Benning, if you know where that is."

"I do. You were an Army brat, I bet."

"Bingo!" he relaxed. "Went from enlistment at Benning, to airborne school, then to the maritime academy where I didn't have to do as many push-ups. You know the rest.

"You probably read my file in your father's office before agreeing to serve with me on the rusty old *Bangor*.

"Now it's your turn to confess. Why didn't you choose one of his sleek, new, comfortable vessels with plenty of young officers attending your every whim?"

She chuckled. "There's your age hang-up showing again, Captain Casey Flynn."

"Speaking of age," he fingered the heavy fabric of her jacket. "Why do you hide yourself under a seaman's work uniform?"

"Stop it! I'm the ship's security officer, not its female gadget!"

"I retract the question. You and I have a mission: finding the murderer or murderers of our crew and preserving what's left of it."

He gestured to her two chairs. "Can we sit and talk? I brought a list of the crew plus a few of their records."

He handed her the papers. "The top two are just-hired replacements named Cruz and Saldana. No records on them as yet. Nor do I have their fingerprints."

She reached into her desk and extracted a large, blank card. "Speaking of that, I need your fingerprints, Captain."

Without hesitation, she inked his fingers and thumbs and pressed them on the card.

"There, that didn't hurt, did it?"

He studied the clear imprints she had made on the card. "You're good."

Wiping his fingers, he almost added 'For a female,' but wisely chose not to.

"What else?" she looked up from the crew records.

"A diagram of the main deck," he handed her a sketch. "The x's indicate where Seaman Creech should have walked on patrol. The double x's mark where the First Mate discovered a smudge of blood on the railing the next morning, but no Creech."

She nodded. "Not too late to check for fingerprints. Do we have Creech's?"

Casey fumbled with the crew records. "Yeah, here is his fingerprint card.

"This may not be the best time but I'm curious about your records. Born in Barbados?"

"Yes, Captain," she sighed. "I might as well get this out of the way, presuming you're interested."

"I am."

"Well, I have doting parents, mother is dead and you know my father. I have no brothers or sisters, which--you're thinking--makes me a spoiled brat."

"No, ma'm," Casey protested. "I find you both delightful and professional."

She continued in a monotone. "Normal upbringing and schooling in Bridgetown. Attended the university there and studied economics and business."

She paused. "Is that enough?"

Casey grinned. "Except the question all interviewers ask, 'What position do you intend to hold in five years?'"

She studied him a moment before replying. "I expect to be your boss in less than two years, Captain."

CHAPTER FIVE

S IDE BY SIDE, they walked down to the galley on the next deck. Alonzo, the short, bushy-haired cook, stood there leaning on a mop.

He wore soiled cook's whites, and a grey mushroom-shaped cap. His other exposed anatomy was lightly dusted with enriched flour and imaginative tattoos.

Alonzo declined shaking hands with Kathlee. "I'll get flour all over you," he backed away, studying his new captain and security officer.

"Hope you two are big eaters," he mumbled. "We loaded lots of grub in Singapore."

He scrubbed a spot on the deck. "Ma'm, since you're our security officer, what happened to Creech?

"All of a sudden he disappeared. Did he jump ship in Singapore?"

"We're still looking for him," Kathlee replied first. "Singapore police are searching but haven't told us anything as yet."

"Ah…" Alonzo turned aside. "Excuse me. The bread smells done."

"Most everyone has a nickname here," Flynn led her to the rail. "Alonzo's nickname is 'Papa.'"

"He's a father?"

"Maybe. But 'papa' also means potato."

As they entered the mess together, heads turned in unison

to stare at the striking security officer accompanied by their new captain.

"Men, this is our new Security Officer, Miss Sigmund," Flynn announced needlessly and began introducing the others.

A wiry tall man from the opposite end of the mess table stood. "I'm Seaman Gary Park, also known as 'Speedy.'"

He was a muscular, bearded young man with tattooed arms and long braided hair kept in place with rubber bands.

"Next is Seaman 'Hoosier' Hauser," Flynn said. A serious young man wearing thick glasses nodded, reminding Sigmund of a first year university student.

"You saw our first engineer, Karl Friauf, at work below but didn't actually meet him." Friauf waved a hand from the other end of the table.

"Sit here, Miss Sigmund," Casey held a chair. "We dine family style and everyone passes dishes around the table. No formality here, as you see, unlike your father's fine dining room in Bridgetown."

To hide her frown at the mention of her father, she looked around, counting. "This our whole crew?"

"No," Casey replied. "We have to eat in shifts since we are so few. Only twelve males at the moment, we need to recruit more."

He passed an empty plate to Kathlee, then handed her utensils wrapped in a napkin. Casey held a pot of stew and almost over-filled her plate before he stopped, embarrassed.

"Sorry," he murmured.

"Thank you, Captain," she grinned at his discomfort. "Pass the salt, please."

Later, Friauf excused himself, saying "I'm beat and my shift starts at midnight."

The other men began drifting away, also claiming duty or rest. Casey and Kathlee were the only ones left at the long table.

"Well," she began. "They seem…"

He stopped her with a finger to his lips and motioned they should leave the mess.

At the rail outside, he whispered, "I think we should talk privately only in one of our cabins. I've searched both of them several times for hidden listening devices. If there are killers aboard, we've got to be cautious."

Inside his cabin there was only a narrow bed, table, bureau and two chairs. Flynn placed the chairs on opposite sides of the table and held her chair.

"No formality, Captain," she chided, "either in the mess or your cabin."

He sat and folded his hands, grinning at her rebuke. "What are your impressions of our First Mate?"

She replied with a question. "Why wasn't he there, in the mess?"

"He was at the police station checking again on our missing seaman." He repeated, "What do you think of First Mate Avery?"

"May I smoke?" she asked, before tossing a cigarette pack on the table.

He nodded. "Any other bad habits? Back to Avery."

She answered after lighting a cigarette. "He strikes me as an organizer, probably the focal point and accepted boss of your crew. Previous navy experience, I'm guessing."

"You must have read his record, along with mine, before accepting this job." Flynn questioned and lit one of her cigarettes. "The next man you met in the mess was Gary Park. Your opinion of Park?"

"Sure, I saw your record and Avery's, too," she admitted. "According to my father, you're the hero of the *Mayaguez* seizure by the Cambodians and deserve a gold medal."

"Not true," Flynn coughed. "Back to Park. What about him?"

She studied him before responding. "Modest, eh? That's another plus.

"About Park, he seems a bit nervous and skittish. I'd say he feels pressure and stress more than the average sailor. Anything you want to share with me about his record?"

"He has a common problem among us seamen," Flynn studied his hands.

"Alcohol, drugs, women?"

Flynn nodded. "Your first guess, Security Officer. Moving on, what's your impression of Seaman 'Hoosier' Houser?"

"He should be at home in Indiana, studying for his final exams. Hands too soft for a seaman."

"Our first engineer, Karl Friauf?"

She stubbed out the cigarette in the ashtray he offered. "Seems capable, probably reliable."

"Next, Alonzo, our cook. Any concerns?"

"None. Dinner, especially that stew and biscuits, were delicious. I'll have to watch my weight. He's a great one-man kitchen."

"No revelations, Captain," she later stood and stretched. "Once it's dark, why don't we shadow the deck detail since that's where Creech went missing? Unless you have a better idea?"

He also stretched before sitting again. "That's a start. Since we have a little time until dark, there is one other person we need to consider."

"Who?"

"You, Security Officer Sigmund," he leaned forward, touching her hand. "Why are you here in this unimportant oil tanker instead of on one of your father's giant transports?"

She crossed her arms defensively, and made a face. "I'm here to learn the marine transport business established by my hard-working father. He built *Seatrans* from scratch, starting with a single ketch in Bridgetown.

"If I'm to eventually succeed him--and I shall--I must know the business backward and forward. The best place to begin is on a small vessel like the *Bangor*.

"That satisfy you, Captain?"

Casey Flynn held up his hands in surrender. "Partially, ma'm, only partially. I look forward to hearing more later, especially the non-duty, hidden side of Security Officer Kathlee Sigmund."

Ignoring him, she jumped to her feet. "Time we visited the bridge with new orders to turn on the deck lights at intervals during the darkness. That should improve the deck guards' protection. Think you can handle those steep stairs again?"

He looked startled. "Of course I can. Why do you ask?"

"Didn't I notice you limping earlier? Your time for confession."

"You're very alert," he acknowledged. "Great trait for either a security officer or head of a giant transport company.

"I must be more careful around you, ma'm."

"How were you injured, Captain?"

"Hate to admit it, but I broke an ankle on my last parachute jump at Benning."

Climbing up to the bridge together, they met a man hurrying down.

Flynn caught the man's arm. "Security Officer Sigmund, this is Second Mate Tejada."

"Yes, I've already had the pleasure. Conejo picked me up at the airport."

"Oh, of course! Conejo, who's left on the bridge?"

Tejada paled. "Just going to the can, sir. Won't be a moment."

Flynn frowned. "The helmsman better not be up there alone!

"Go!" He told Tejada, who scurried down the companionway.

To Kathlee, Flynn said, "Let's meet Smitty, our helmsman."

Smitty looked up as they entered the bridge. A short, gray-haired veteran, he shyly bobbed his head, upon introduction.

"Where did the Second Mate go in such a hurry?"

Smitty shook his head. "Said he'd forgotten something important, Captain, and went down to fetch it."

Captain and Security Officer exchanged looks.

Remembering why they were there, Casey asked "Can you see any part of the main deck at night from the bridge?"

"No, sir. Can't see hardly anything on the deck unless the lights are on. Normally, the lights are off, to preserve our night vision."

"You can control those lights from the bridge?"

"Yes, sir."

"Show us, please."

Smitty obliged at an electrical panel across from the control console. The main deck immediately sparkled with light.

"Thanks, Smitty. That's fine. Turn them off."

As they descended from the bridge, they met Tejada on his way up.

"Had to go to the head, Captain, in a hurry. I'm okay now."

On the darkened main deck they walked toward the bow and met another crewman securing the gangway, preparatory to embarking.

"Partagas, this is Security Officer Sigmund."

"Pancho Partagas, ma'm. Glad to know ya'."

As they shook hands. Flynn asked, "Anything amiss, Pancho? The cook told me he loaned everyone a kitchen knife for personal security. Did you get one?"

Partagas withdrew a long knife from his belt. "Yes, sir. Here's mine."

"Fine, Partagas."

Kathlee studied Flynn in the dim light. "Do you have any police batons on board?"

"Great idea. I'll check with Supply. Want to issue them?"

Kathlee tried to read his expression. "Might be a better self-defense weapon than a kitchen knife.

"I could give everyone a class on the use of the baton," she offered.

"I'd like to attend myself," he gestured.

"No, I'm serious," he replied to her expression.

"Raise a ruckus if you have any problem, Pancho," she instructed as they rounded the bow, seeking the other guard on the port side.

"Come here, Saldana," Flynn called. "It's the captain and security officer."

A gangly young man whose curly locks covered his forehead, cautiously approached.

"Saldana is one of our two new replacements," Flynn explained. "Just joined us in Singapore. This is Security Officer Sigmund, Saldana."

Sigmund spoke, hoping to ease the young man's obvious tension. "How's your first day aboard the *Bangor?* Anything you need?"

Saldana's reply sounded strained. "No, ma'm. Takes getting used to, you know, out here alone in the dark."

"Well, remember that Partagas is over there on the starboard. He'd appreciate it if you kept in touch by calling out to him when you pass."

"You might time it so you reach the bow with Partagas at about the same time," Flynn suggested.

"Call out if you need help…or anything," Kathlee added as she and Flynn continued toward the stern.

On the way below, to the engine room, she asked, "Don't you have I-phones? The night watchmen could communicate that way, too."

He motioned to the bulkheads. "All this steel interferes."

"Unless you have line-of-sight," she caught herself, at his expression. "You're right. I-phones don't always work well. We tried them in Bridgetown."

Arms folded, Flynn faced her. "Let's meet the Second Engineer, Franz Suppe, whom you've not even seen."

She followed him, descending into the engine room. "Suppe can teach you how to operate our diesels." Casey said. "Fascinating subject for a lady just out of university."

She stopped. "Good memory, Captain. I must remember that."

"Watch your step!" He grabbed her as she lurched forward. "This can be as slippery as a new captain."

She stared at his hand on her arm. "Thanks, Captain. You're already teaching me to be extra cautious."

Next to the engine control panels, they found Second Engineer Suppe and another man sitting on folding chairs. Flynn named them both for her.

"This is Cruz, the other replacement hired in Singapore. He's had previous experience with diesels so he's assisting Franz and Karl."

She nodded at both men. "You'll see me down here often, trying to understand how you engineers keep this old vessel afloat."

Tall, dark-headed Suppe stood. "You're welcome at any time, ma'm. Being down here we're separated from the others most of the day.

"It gets lonely and we always wonder what's happening topside."

"Well, topside is quiet today," she spoke first. "Let's hope it continues."

"Cruz," Flynn asked, "are you settled-in okay? Need anything?"

The new replacement raised a hand to his mouth as if hesitant to speak. Short and solid, he succeeded in nodding at both of them.

Finally, he responded. "Everything's fine, sir. Trying to get used to my new job and new mates."

A concerned expression lit Cruz's face. "Is it true that a crewman is missing?"

Flynn hesitated, but answered. "True, Cruz. We don't know where he is at the moment."

"That's why each of us must be alert at all times," Sigmund added. "We don't want to lose anyone else."

CHAPTER SIX

THE BRIDGE, DECK and engine room were particularly active as lines were winched aboard, turbines revved, and the ship klaxon sounded, alerting the Port of Singapore they were leaving. The *Bangor* was steaming west into the Strait of Malacca and its next destination.

Captain Flynn stood near the control console where he could watch both console and the actions of the helmsman and First Mate. Security Officer Sigmund stood aside, studying every action.

Topside in the mess, the midnight shift was assembling for instructions before beginning its all-night duty. Most of the men puffed cigarettes or pipes and drank black coffee from a steaming pot on the mess table.

"Three to one, I'm betting!"

Seaman Park waved a fifty dollar bill aloft. "The next man to go into the drink and not come back will be…?"

"Smitty!" someone wagered.

"Naw," Park shook his head. "It will be that new man on deck watch tonight. What's his name?"

"Saldana," someone called out the name.

"Little Miss Security Officer will keep us all safe," another man chuckled. "But you'd better keep your distance from her, like the Captain said."

A louder voice objected. "I never heard him say that!"

"She can't guard us all the time." Houser crushed a

cigarette into a butt can. "I agree with Park. The next missing man will be Saldana."

"Money up, then!"

"Before we reach the next port, George Town, we'll lose another mate, probably Saldana. That's my bet!"

"Here's my fifty, but on Cruz, the other newbie!"

"I'm betting fifty dollars, it'll be you, Park. That is, if you have the guts to go out on the dark deck tonight!"

In the following hubbub, paper and pencil were provided to record the bets. The resultant stack of dollar bills kept growing.

First Mate Avery rapped on the captain's door.

Flynn opened the door, surveying the empty passageway.

"Come in and tell me how the crew's feeling."

"About our missing seaman, Captain?"

"Certainly that and what they think about our new security officer."

Avery removed his visor cap and sat, rubbing his sparse red hair. "Well, the crew's a mite upset, talking and wondering what happened to Seaman Creech."

"I wish we knew he is alive somewhere. That all?"

"No, sir. They're afeared of who'll be next. Truthfully, sir, each man is afraid it may be him!"

The Captain and First Mate lit cigarettes from the pack left by Sigmund. "If there is a murderer in our crew, who do you suspect, First Mate?"

"Dunno, Captain. All I have is a quirky feeling that something's about to happen. Maybe something really bad."

Flynn leaned forward, encouraging a reply. "Who is it?"

"Must be someone in the deck section," Avery began.

"Could be Park," he continued. "Never trusted him since I got him out of jail in St. George's. You know he's alcoholic?"

Flynn leaned back in his chair. "Yeah, I heard about his habit. Tell me this, why would anyone want to kill a mate on our ship? There would have to be a motive, a whale of a motive."

"Maybe someone knows you got six months of pay locked up in that safe there." The First Mate gestured to the big, iron box in the corner.

"Well," Flynn exhaled, "I'm at a loss at what to do. Maybe we should put someone watching Park?"

"We're short-handed, Captain. Sounds like a chore for that new security officer." Avery grinned, knowing Flynn wouldn't risk the daughter of the line's president.

"No, First Mate. You've got to be our eyes and ears. Naturally, I'll do the same. I'll even tell Sigmund what we've thinking.

"But I'm depending on you, First Mate. Keep your eyes open! Frequent reports!"

"Aye, aye, sir"

Later, Kathlee sat in Flynn's cabin, as he shared the First Mate's suspicions. "Here's an idea, Security Officer."

She interrupted. "First, Captain, I must tell you that Sparks just received a message from the Singapore police. They report there's still no sign of Seaman Creech, alive or dead. I think we've got to presume he went overboard and is dead."

"Does the crew know about that message?"

"No, sir."

Flynn took a deep breath. "Ah… would you mind if I called you Kathlee when we're alone like this?"

"Does the favor extend to your security officer, Captain?

"It does."

"Then my answer is 'yes, Casey."

That accomplished, Casey grinned, pleased at her answer to his hesitant question.

"I'll patrol the main deck tonight until daylight…"

"No, no," she exclaimed. "We split it, Casey. I'll take it until 0100 hours, after that it's your turn."

'No, ma'm. How do I explain to your father why I allowed you to be endangered? You, out on deck at night by yourself, looking for a murderer? Hell, no!

"What I need from you, Kathlee, are your thoughts. Why would anyone want to eliminate our crew? Why take over a twelve-year old, rusty tanker once everyone's out of the way?

"Why? What's the reason? Is there something of great value aboard the *Bangor* that we don't know about?"

She sat for a moment, staring at him. "Get the manifest out of the safe. Maybe there's a clue there that's not apparent to us two newbies."

"Okay," he conceded. "I'll send for our supper here. Afterwards, I'll get you the manifest. You examine it while I'm patrolling the main deck. Later we'll compare findings."

"If any."

"Okay, if any. We've got to start somewhere."

Kathlee stood. "Somewhere better be my cabin. I'm spending too much time in yours. How will I know it's you?"

"Good point! I'll knock like this. Dum, de, dum, dum. But don't wait up."

He pointed at her bunk. "Get some rest."

She responded with a snappy salute. "Yes…Casey!"

CHAPTER SEVEN

IN HIS CABIN early the next morning, she thrust a cup of coffee into his hands. "I didn't hear any 'Dum, de, dum, dum' last night. How'd it go?"

Flynn sat up, rubbing his forehead and holding a blanket over his chest.

"All was quiet. Park and Houser were on deck with me, but not together. They like being armed with your batons.

"Thanks for the coffee."

"Like it? I brewed it in my cabin," she bragged. "If you're up to it, here's the manifest to go over after your crew meeting.

In the mess upstairs, more coffee was being poured from the big pot and cigarettes lit before the half-crew meeting began. The smoke almost obscured the big map behind the captain.

The First Mate shook his head at Flynn's look, meaning nothing new to report.

Flynn stood in front of the large scale map. "We're presently at this position," he pointed, "about two days out of our next refueling job in George Town.

"We'll make our delivery there by midday, day after tomorrow."

He turned to Friauf, the chief engineer. "How are things below, Karl?"

"The engines are operating steady and strong, Captain. No

problem making George Town as long as the good weather and our hull welds hold."

Everyone snickered at his joke.

Seaman Smithson held up a hand. "Captain?"

"Yes, Smitty?"

Smithson coughed. "It's that we're working double shifts, sir."

Many other heads nodded agreement.

"Captain, we can't keep this up indefinitely without rest."

The First Mate stood, staring down Smithson. "Smitty, the Captain's well aware of that. He plans to give us time off as soon as we've unloaded at George Town. Right, Captain?"

Flynn nodded. "I know you are all overworked and appreciate your extra efforts the last several days. As you know, we're understaffed due to our...losses.

"The Second Mate and I are going ashore at George Town to hire more crewmen.

"Any more questions?"

No more hands in the air.

"Then let's get back to work," Flynn ordered. "Stay alert. Stay safe."

Partagas groused quietly as they filed out the door. "Easy for him to stay safe!

"How do we stay safe with a murderer somewhere on board?"

CHAPTER EIGHT

S HE AND CASEY took their usual chairs in her small cabin. "Here's the manifest," she pushed it across the table. "See if you can make anything of it."

Casey paged through the sheaf of papers. Then did it again.

"Nothing here raises the hackles," he shook his head. "Do you see anything?"

"Nothing," she agreed. "But our big hold--even the oil tanks--could be loaded with hidden contraband, drugs... or something." She raised her hands in frustration.

"What would you have done on the *Mayaguez?*"

He stretched. "I'd explore the entire hold carefully with one of the engineers."

"While I make an unannounced inspection of the crew quarters," she countered. "Maybe I'll find a hidden cache of drugs in the shower drains."

Suddenly he sat up straight. "Not without me."

She frowned. "Stop that! I'm the security officer, inspecting where and when I like."

She quickly changed the challenge to a question. "Are we ready for patrolling the main deck tonight?"

He frowned. "Not we...me! You are our strategist, our thinker. I don't want to constantly worry about your safety, Security Officer."

She was studying a small wooden case on her table, opening and closing its lid.

He leaned forward. "What's that?"

She handed it to him. "This is the keenest thing my father ever gave me. It's the old brass directional magnetic compass he used for years on his ketch.

"Be careful. It's delicate, even has a folding sundial. Dad gave it to me to make my first solo voyage to Grenada.

"He told me he was in his ketch by himself one day when a tropical storm struck and pushed him into the forbidden triangle. Know where that is?"

"Sure. It's that area in the Caribbean where compasses are unpredictable due to strange magnetic interference. Lots of ships have been lost in the triangle. Even a flight of U.S. Navy aircraft disappeared there once during the war without a trace."

Flynn examined the compass carefully. "I've never seen a compass like this."

She took it from him. "This compass enabled my father to find his way out of that mysterious triangle, despite the storm, safely back to Bridgetown. That's why it is the best gift he ever gave me! I prize it!

"I intend to pass it on to my son, if I have one, someday."

Casey studied her intently. "I'm sure you will, Kathlee Sigmund. I'm sure you will."

After staring at him a moment, she sighed. "Better get some rest, Captain. You'll be up all night again."

Later In his cabin next door, Flynn was unable to sleep. Thoughts about a possible killer aboard his first ship and first command, biggest personal responsibility since the *Mayaguez*, kept him tossing in his bunk.

Or was it the daughter next door--entrusted him by her doting father--who kept his eyes wide open at all hours?

A scream awakened him from a fitful nap an hour later. He pulled on dungarees and bolted down the passageway toward the sound.

"What's wrong?"

Park stood outside the crew sleeping bay. "Nothing, sir. Smitty was having another nightmare. He's been waking everyone up lately."

Pushing the others aside, Casey found Smithson sitting on the edge of his bunk.

"I'm sorry!" Smithson mumbled, covering his face. "I dreamed I was alone swimming in black water, barely afloat, and the ship was leaving me behind.

"It was terrible!"

Gasping for breath, Kathlee and Suppe, the second engineer, joined the crowd. After hearing Smitty's outburst, she noticed Flynn's tight-fitting dungarees.

"I see we'd better search the clothing locker for a larger size for you, Captain."

Flynn ignored her. "It's alright. Smitty just had a nightmare. Everybody back to sleep."

The off-duty men returned to their bunks. Loudly, someone muttered, "Nobody sleeps easy on the *Bangor* any more."

On the bridge, Second Mate Tejada sat at the console while Captain Flynn and the First Mate pored over charts of the Malay Peninsula's jagged coast line.

Avery dangled calipers in one hand while poking a finger on the chart.

"That's where an Australian freighter grounded last year, Captain. Took two tugs to pull her off that shoal."

Flynn studied the chart. "We're well west of there. Keep a sharp eye on our port, Mr. Tejada."

"Aye, aye, sir," Tejada responded.

"By the way, did you hear a scream up here from somewhere below a few minutes ago?"

"Not a thing, Captain." Tejada patted the stand-by

generator next to the console. "Gets pretty noisy up here when everything's running."

Accompanied by Partagas the next morning, Kathlee inspected the crew quarters, exploring all common-use areas, showers, heads and day room.

Exasperated by her failure to find drugs or weapons, she told Partagas to return to his regular duties.

> *I should be pleased I found nothing suspicious.*
> *Get a grip, neophyte!*

Deciding to reward herself with a fresh cup of coffee from the galley, she entered and extracted a clean cup from the tray. After filling it, she sat on a bench.

From the galley she heard Alonzo, the cook, chanting an old Wailers tune.

> *Emancipate yourself from mental slavery,*
> *None but ourselves can free our minds!*
> *Have no fear of atomic energy,*
> *'Cause none of them can stop the time.*

Papa Alonzo pushed through the double doors with a tray of silverware. "Sorry, Miss! Didn't mean to startle you!"

She turned to watch him stack the silverware. "I like that tune, Papa. You seem to be the happiest man aboard the ship this morning."

She raised her cup to him. "Your coffee is excellent."

"Thank you, Miss"

"Alonzo, why is it you don't seem frightened like the others? Everyone acts afraid of something most of the time. They don't even talk to each other, much less sing."

He wiped his hands on the apron. "It's because they think that man Creech was murdered and tossed overboard.

"There's even a gaming pool to guess who will be the next man to go overboard like Creech."

Piqued, she set down the cup. "Who is the leading candidate, Papa?"

"Don't know, don't want to know, Miss. But it ain't me!"

"How do you know?"

"Easy, Miss. The killer knows if there's no cook, there's no eat! I'm as safe as Bob Marley in his grave."

She knocked at Casey's cabin door. Hearing no reply, she entered, balancing another hot cup of coffee.

"Come on. Get up, Casey!"

He sat up, wiping his eyes, blinking and trying to conceal himself with the blanket. "Thanks for the coffee."

He joked. "You are an exceptional security officer. I'll be certain to highlight your excellent coffee service on your fitness report."

She stuck out her tongue at him. "Just don't spill the coffee on yourself, lord and master."

He took a swallow. "I was about to tell you that my tour on deck ended at about 0500 hours and was uneventful.

"Did your inspection of the crew quarters turn up anything other than a few naughty magazines?

"Today we make port and while unloading, I'll try recruiting new men for our depleted crew. I'm going with the Second Mate. We hope to bring back several good recruits."

CHAPTER NINE

TWO MEN STOOD at the stern, smoking and watching scavenger birds diving for fish in the ship's wake. "Nothing last night. Why?"

"The Captain seemed to be everywhere I wanted to be."

"Maybe he won't be so alert tonight. Can't keep his eyes open all the time."

Glancing about to see they were still alone, the other man joked. "He'll get a real rest soon. Real soon!"

Twirling their new batons, Houser and Partagas stood on the fantail on deck watch.

"How's the 'who's next' pool going?"

"You mean the murder pool?"

"That's it!"

"Cruz was in the lead last I heard. Don't know if anyone is even close to him in the betting."

Relieved, Saldana stammered. "Wh…why Cruz?"

Houser could barely make out the other's face in the dark. "Because he's new and doesn't know his way around. Doesn't have a lot of buddies yet, either."

"Just like me," Saldana exhaled. "I'm new. I must be high on that betting list, too."

"Could be," Houser responded. Saldana stood so close to him, Houser could smell stale breath.

"I'm new, too," Saldana repeated, shuffling his feet. "I'm probably next to Cruz on that list, don't you think?"

Saldana spit over the side. "If I die and you win, what will you do with all that money in the pot?"

Houser turned, suddenly alert and pointed with his baton. "Did ya' hear something over there?"

"Didn't hear nothing," Saldana scoffed. "You trying to scare me?"

"Well...I heard something," Houser persisted. "I'm going over to the port rail and check that noise."

"See you later," Saldana said, then hissed at Houser's back. "Don't try to scare me again!"

On the deck an hour later, Flynn touched Houser's shoulder. "Where's Saldana?"

Taken by surprise, Houser squeaked, "Over on the port side, Captain."

"How long has it been since you've seen or heard from him?"

Houser checked his luminous wrist watch. "Probably a half hour, sir."

"Come with me," Flynn half-ran to the other side, pulling out an I-phone to tell the bridge to turn on all the deck lights and sound the klaxon.

The off-duty crew, led by the First Mate, quickly gathered on the lighted deck. Meanwhile, Flynn searched the port rail where Saldana should have been.

Back to the group, he silently held up Saldana's baton by its leather thong.

"Found this in the scrupper near the deck house."

He handed it to the just-arrived Security Officer.

"I'll bag it later," she nodded.

"Action!" he said, looking at the First Mate.

"Let's search the ship top to bottom to make sure Saldana didn't go to the can…or something."

"I'll take the bottom," Kathlee volunteered. Searching the faces around her, she motioned for Friauf, Cruz and Partagas to follow her below.

The First Mate spoke up. "Smithson and Park, come with me. We'll search the decks and bridge castle."

An hour later, the search was competed. Judging from the searchers' somber faces, they found no trace of Saldana.

Flynn faced them. "Please follow me to the mess, everyone. The Security Officer and I are going to interview each of you. Please sit apart at the table. Do not talk to anyone about anything!

"We'll call you individually to the day room for interview."

The First Mate stepped into the day room and sat down, facing them.

He struck the table with his fist. "I don't understand how a sailor--even a new one--can disappear without a trace, sir.

"You know, don't you, that everyone will claim innocence? These interviews are a waste of time!"

Sigmund raised her eyebrows. "If you have a better idea of how to proceed, tell us."

The First Mate turned toward her. "I told you my suspicions already. It's that damned drunkard, Park. See him next. Force him to confess what he's done with Creech…and now Saldana!"

"We ask the questions, First Mate. You answer them," Flynn fumed.

Kathlee placed a small recorder on the table. "Let's go ahead and get your answers to our questions, First Mate. The sooner we get your statement about your whereabouts the last thirty minutes, the better.

"Speak into the microphone here," she pointed. "Now, do you have any objection to your statement being recorded?"

Avery leaned back in the chair, shaking his head.

"You must speak, First Mate. Answer the question!"

"No objection."

Sigmund began. "Where were you at midnight, First Mate, when the klaxon sounded? Speak slowly and distinctly."

"In my quarters," he shrugged. "When I heard the alarm, I ran down to the deck. The Captain said Saldana was missing and we searched for him topside. No luck," he shook his head.

"Were you alone in your quarters?"

"Of course. Yes."

"Did you see anyone on your way to the deck?"

"The Second Mate and I came down together."

Sigmund took a deep breath. "Do you have any knowledge who is responsible for the missing Saldana…or Creech?"

Red-faced, Avery answered. "I told you already. It is that drunkard, Park!"

Nodding he could leave, Kathlee clicked off the recorder.

Second Mate Conejo Tejada knocked at the door. "Can I be next? My shift starts in twenty minutes."

Kathlee repeated the preparatory sentences. "Where were you, Second Mate, when the alarm sounded? What were your actions at that time?"

"I was on my bunk, trying to sleep."

"And?"

"I got dressed and went down to the main deck where you," he indicated the Captain, "were assembling the crew."

"You came to the main deck directly from your cabin?"

He rubbed rheumy eyes. "Yes, ma'm."

"Did you hear or see anything unusual on your way to the deck?"

"I saw the First Mate and we came down together. No, I didn't hear anything unusual."

Flynn reminded Tejada his answers were being recorded. "So they better be truthful."

"Have you any knowledge about the identity of the murderer of Saldana or Creech?"

"No, ma'm."

"Or any suspicions about who the murderer is?"

"No, ma'm."

"I'm surprised. As our second mate, you must have insights about each and every man in our crew."

Tejada flustered. "That's right, ma'm. I know a lot about everybody."

"Have you any inkling who the murderer is--who's killing our crew--one by one?"

The door banged open and Partagas burst in, breathless.

"Come quick, Captain! There's a big fight in the mess!"

CHAPTER TEN

Pushing open the mess door, Flynn was the first inside. Two men writhed on the floor. The First Mate stood over them, cursing and trying to separate them.

"Stop it!" Flynn snarled, grabbing each man by the collar. "Stand up!" He stood between them to keep them apart.

"Who started this?" He looked at the First Mate for an answer.

First Mate Avery straightened his cap before pointing. "Cruz accused Park of killing his buddy, Saldana."

"I didn't!" Park wiped his bloody nose on a sleeve. "I didn't do nothing and he knows it!"

Cruz pointed at Park. "He's crazy, Captain! Crazy!"

Flynn, joined by Sigmund, surveyed the others in the room. "The rest of you, sit down and keep quiet until we call for you. No talking!"

With that, Flynn motioned Park and Cruz out the door and into the dayroom.

Turning on the recorder, Kathlee resumed her seat. "Your answers are being recorded, so tell the truth, both of you."

Admiring her composure, Flynn sat beside her and studied the two sailors. "Okay, Cruz. Tell us why you think Park killed Saldana."

Chest heaving, Cruz glared at Park, then back at Flynn. "He has it in for Saldana and me 'cause we're replacements."

"Not true," Park retorted before Flynn could stop him.

"Quiet, Park! You'll get your turn."

He turned back to Cruz. "Again my question. Why do you think Park killed your buddy? You must have a better reason than 'he doesn't like us.'"

Cruz pointed a shaking finger at Park. "He bet everyone that Saldana would be the next man missing."

"Park, did you do that?"

"I didn't mean anything by it," Park panted. "It was a hunch that's all. We were all placing bets on one another."

"A hunch that he," Cruz pointed again, "made happen so he would win the pool. That's why he killed Saldana, to win all that money!"

"What pool?"

"He jokes that it's the 'murder pool.'"

"If you don't stop him," Cruz pointed again, "I'll be the next killed!"

Flynn returned Cruz to the mess. In the hallway between mess and dayroom, he whispered to Kathlee.

> "I need everyone back on duty. This ship can't run itself to George Town. The duty shift has been on for eighteen hours straight."

"Send the others back to work but keep Park for questioning," Kathlee suggested. "The first delivery at George Town is scheduled in five hours. We may have to arrive late. We need all hands for a safe delivery there. Let's try to solve this first."

Returning to the dayroom, Flynn told Park, "Put your knife on the table, Park. I want to see it."

"Did you kill Saldana"

"No, sir! I didn't touch him despite what that crazy Cruz said."

Kathlee gingerly placed the knife in an evidence bag.

"Did you bet the others that Saldana would be the next one missing?"

"The pool is just a game, to pass the time, ma'm! I didn't kill nobody!"

"Stick out you hands, Park," she minutely examined his palms and fingers. "Now we're going to your bunk to look in your wall locker and sea chest."

"Where do we stand now?"

Kathlee and Casey sat at the small table in her cabin. Ordered not to move, Park was next door in the sick bay.

She frowned. "There's nothing incriminating in his gear."

"Nor blood on his knife, hands or fingernails?"

"Nothing, Casey."

"What do you think about Park?"

She shifted in her chair. "I don't think Park is our murderer. Let's put him back to work in the deck section."

Casey admired her azure eyes. "Agree."

He checked his watch. "We'll be docking at the George Town terminal in two hours. Until then we can interview the rest of the crew, one at a time, right here.

"If that's alright with you, Kathlee," he added.

For an hour and half, before Flynn had to be on the bridge, they called the crewmen not yet interviewed into the cabin. After all statements were recorded, they reviewed and discussed the responses.

Casey looked despondent. "From my experiences on the *Mayaguez*, all these statements are tainted. I'm sure they talked to one another after we left."

She stood and stretched. "That fight might even have been staged to throw off us off the murderer."

"Good point," Casey agreed. "Park or Cruz may have just wanted to muddle their crewmates' memories."

"Maybe both Park and Cruz."

She held up three fingers. "Park, Smithson and Partagas, their statements seem to confirm their whereabouts at midnight.

"Friauf and Houser claim they were sleeping. One or both of them could have been on the main deck."

"Second Mate Tejada was on duty on the bridge. That seems to clear him."

Flynn sighed. "But we saw how easily he left the bridge that first night, didn't we?"

"Alonzo, the cook, was in the galley, preparing early breakfast for the shift. Franz Suppe, our second engineer, was on duty, alone, in the engine room."

Kathlee threw up both hands. "We're getting nowhere! What can we do differently, Casey?"

"On the bright side," he tried to cheer her, "We eliminated the 'murder pool' and returned their money to the bettors. We prohibited any future pools on the *Bangor*."

"That's a start, but we still have an unknown killer in our midst.

"Casey, do you remember the first question we had for the First Mate?"

"About whom he suspects?"

"Un-huh. It's interesting that he lied about that."

Casey checked his watch. "Let's listen to that tape again. I don't recall his exact wording."

"As a precaution, can you alert the George Town police to have a few uniforms within hailing distance when we unload the fuel? We can't afford to lose anyone jumping ship there."

She reached for his hand. "And then?"

"I must get to the bridge. See you later?"

He stopped at the door. "Be extra careful, please?"

CHAPTER ELEVEN

T HE CAPTAIN AND Security Officer stood in the mast house the next morning, surveying the activity below. They watched the workmen ashore attach the ship's big cargo hoses to George Town's shore pier.

Casey pointed to the workers. "They're hooking up our number two tank. Lots of activity aboard precedes a hook-up. The ship must remain in constant balance as a tank is depleted. We must observe really strict safety precautions prior to and during the discharge."

Kathlee, just returned from police headquarters where she'd reported Saldana missing, nodded at Casey's explanation. She motioned to a group of sweating deck hands.

"Look...Even our suspect, Park, is busy this morning."

"Did you return him his knife?"

"I did. If he's innocent of Saldana's disappearance or death, he may need to protect himself from the real killer in our midst."

"Don't we all?" Casey mused aloud.

"All, that is, except you, Kathlee."

To her look of annoyance, he added. "Your father figure-- that's me--intends to protect you all the way home to Bridgetown or wherever you want to go."

She laughed. "Who protects me from the father figure?"

He spoke in her ear because of the noisy clamor of whistles, voices and signals on deck. "Amazing!"

She backed away. "What?"

"You! You are a marvelous combination of technical expertise, inquiring mind and humor. Besides being lovely in a seaman's sweater and…"

A shout from the men at the cargo manifold stifled Casey's last words.

"I'd better check below with Karl Friauf," Casey picked up the telephone. Friauf promptly reported he was manipulating the ballast tanks as usual to keep the ship in trim, and constantly monitoring and adjusting pressure gauges.

Another telephone call was for Kathlee. "I'm needed in the sick bay," she called over her shoulder as she left.

Alonzo, the cook, stood in the hallway outside the sick bay, waving a large butcher knife. Apoplectic, he pointed the knife at a shattered door.

"Look, Miss!

"I found it like this when I finished feeding breakfast," he stuttered. "Thought I should call you or the Captain right away."

"You did exactly right, Alonzo," she assured him. After examining the damaged door she warily stepped inside.

Inside she glanced about the room and went directly to a mangled medicine cabinet. It had been splintered, its contents--medicine bottles and vials of liquids--lay in sparkling shards of glass all over the floor.

Casey came through the door, side-stepped Alonzo, and stopped so suddenly he bumped into Kathlee. "Sorry! Can you tell what's missing?"

"Sure," she said, motioning Alonzo into the hall. "No need to inventory. The obvious target was drugs. Whoever it was, took all of this one," she held up an empty box.

"Fentanyl," she read the label aloud.

"A narcotic? To be sold ashore or used here?"

"Yeah, a narcotic," she studied the label again. "Moreover, a dangerous one. It can kill!"

She extracted an inventory sheet from the shattered cabinet. "This box is small but it apparently contained," she read, "twelve individually-sealed 200 microgram pills."

She grimaced. "If a person swallowed a few pills, he'd lose consciousness…maybe even die.

"Why would we have so much of this dangerous narcotic on our vessel?"

"Don't know," Casey studied her. "I need a cup of coffee to calm me down,"

"Me, too," she gestured to her cabin. "I brewed a pot earlier."

After they sat down with filled cups, Casey muttered "What else can go wrong? We have two crewmen murdered by an unknown killer. Now we have lethal drugs somewhere aboard and a short-handed, very unhappy crew busily unloading cargo!"

"Maybe whoever took the drugs didn't have time to hide them well. We'll immediately search the ship," she refilled their cups.

"I'll have to report the drug loss to the local police," she placed chin in hand.

"By the way," he forced a smile, "once the report of our latest murder gets around town, the recruitment pool, if there is one, will dry up."

"Guess we have no alternative to another search," they nodded at each other.

"The drugs could be anywhere," Casey groused. "This is like searching for a feather in a chicken factory."

She paused at her door. "If you're not up to it, I'll handle it myself."

He made a face. "No, you won't! The First Mate can handle the rest of the unloading. I'm going with you.

"First, let me make a call over the ship-to-shore line. Shouldn't take more than a minute, then we'll begin the search. Together."

Later, after an unsuccessful search for drugs, unloading tank number two and deck cargo for George Town, Flynn ordered the helmsman to steer past the breakwater and back into the Strait of Malacca.

"Captain, you promised the crew some time off," the First Mate reminded him.

"Sorry, First Mate, but they can rest six miles out, as readily as in port," Flynn frowned as Kathlee entered the bridge and heard the bad news about shore leave.

"We can't afford a single deserter," he explained. "No, repeat no, replacements were willing to sign up, according to the Second Mate. Our *Bangor* has earned an unfortunate tag as the 'Murder Ship,' he said.

Flynn shook his head sadly. "I'm surprised our reputation spread so quickly. First Mate, you did check the roll, right?"

"Aye, Captain. All present. Any further orders for the helm, sir?"

Flynn stared at the charts on the console. "Tell Friauf we start for Banda Aceh, our next port, at first light. That gives the crew several hours of rest. Tell Alonzo to fix us all a big, nice supper.

"I hope some extra time off and a good meal will improve the crew's morale. It usually worked on the *Mayaguez*.

"God forbid that we lose any more hands!"

CHAPTER TWELVE

I N THE CREW quarters beneath the bridge, several sailors
sat on bunks in a half-circle, facing each other.

Park and Hauser lit cigarettes while the others passed a
handful of tinfoil packets from one person to another.

"What's this?" Partagas asked when passed the handful.

"I dunno," Cruz hunched his shoulders.

"Where'd it come from?"

No one answered.

"This tinfoil says 'Fentanyl.' Anybody know what that is?"

Someone on the opposite bunk volunteered. "I heard it's
a sleep aid."

Cruz took a closer look. "It also says 'narcotic.'"

Partagas exclaimed, "That's dangerous!"

Another voice added, "And illegal! Whose is it?"

"Who knows? Maybe it was found on deck after we
unloaded."

"Better turn it in to the Security Officer."

Cruz pitched it to his neighbor. "I'm not turning it in and
getting in trouble. I'd never get shore leave again!"

Smithson accused the group. "You're all chicken! Give it
here!

"I'll take care of it." He grabbed the packets and left the bay.

"Besides" he paused, looking back at them, "I haven't been
sleeping good lately. Damn nightmares!"

"Maybe with this stuff I can sleep real well."

Someone called out in alarm. "Don't take that stuff, Smitty. It's a drug! Throw it overboard!"

A man in the far bunk yelled, "We never saw it, did we guys?"

"Right!" they chorused as Smitty slammed the door behind him.

Casey and Kathlee returned to survey the damaged sick bay. "Did Alonzo hear anyone smash in that door?"

"He said no," Casey shook his head. "Nor did anyone on the bridge hear anything unusual."

"I'll dust for fingerprints. There might be some on the cabinet door or on some of that broken glass."

"I think we should search for those drugs first," Casey demurred.

She agreed. "I'll dust in here later. First we'd better look around the crew's quarters for those drugs."

"I've a better place to look," Casey said. "Crew quarters is too obvious a hiding place."

"Then where?"

"Day room, showers, bilge, even this very room, are likely. Maybe even the bridge. Who would expect us to look up there?"

After three hours of searching the "likely" hiding places, a disconsolate captain and security officer again faced each other in her cabin.

Casey looked about the small room. "You keep this place locked, right?"

She nodded. "You told me I had the only key."

A thought struck her. "Tell me, Casey. Who did you call on the ship-to-shore in George Town?"

"Glad you asked. I almost forgot that we have a suspect as a result of that call. I spoke to the maritime employment agency in George Town."

She raised an eyebrow. "And?"

"They said no one from the *Bangor* had been there recruiting seamen. Tejada lied to us about having been there."

Kathlee pursed her lips. "If he wasn't recruiting there, where was he?"

After his all-night walk on the main deck and below, Casey was hard to awaken. Kathlee prodded his shoulder repeatedly.

"Get up, Casey! Big trouble!"

He sat up immediately. "Trouble?"

"Another death."

"Dear God! Who?"

"Get dressed. I'll wait for you in the hall."

Before closing the door, she peeked at the lean, muscled body partially hidden by a blanket. Catching the look, he pulled the blanket closer while fumbling for his shoes.

"You're busted!" he accused.

She retreated to the hall, until a clothed Casey Flynn appeared.

"Where…?"

All business, she pointed. "This way, Captain.

"Partagas found the body in a stall in the head. It's poor Smitty."

Pushing past the seamen crowding around the entrance to the restroom, Flynn ordered the First Mate to take names of the witnesses.

"Send the others to their duty stations. We get underway at daybreak," he reminded.

A babble of questions rose from the group unwilling to leave the scene.

"What happened?"

"Who's dead?"

"Who killed him?"

One agitated voice rang out. "The real question is… who is going to be the next to die on this damned murder ship?"

Casey and Kathlee stood outside the toilet stall, its door held ajar by a half-clothed body. On the floor was a crumpled paper cup and several discarded foil packets.

She winced. "Looks like we found our missing drugs, but too late for Smitty.

"This is a crime scene. Stop! We're walking all over evidence. I'm off to get my camera."

The First Mate thrust his head into the room. "Is he…?"

"Yes, he's dead," Casey responded, but leaned over to check the carotid artery anyway.

"Appears he took the drugs--Security Officer says they are fentanyl--stolen from the medicine cabinet and they killed him."

"Maybe he didn't even know what they were," the First Mate speculated.

"Maybe Smitty didn't even steal them, maybe someone else did. Then gave them to Smitty."

Armed with her camera, Kathlee began taking photos of the scene. She looked up from her work.

"Wasn't it Smitty who's been having those nightmares and keeping everybody awake in the crew bay?"

"You're right!" Casey looked up from searching the body "He could have thought they were sleeping pills and swallowed them by mistake."

"I'll have to interview the men who were with them last night. Someone must have seen him with those drugs."

Casey frowned. "Meanwhile, we've got to get underway, First Mate, for Banda Aceh. We still have a schedule to meet and customers to satisfy, despite these all these deaths!"

CHAPTER THIRTEEN

"**A**NY LUCK WITH Smitty's bunkmates?"

She sat down heavily beside him on the bridge's console bench. Kathlee looked drawn, so Casey fetched a cup of coffee and a cookie for her.

He resisted the urge to massage her back, although she was probably too exhausted to complain.

"None of them admit knowing what Smitty was doing last night. No one even claims to have seen him after supper."

"Do you believe them?"

"No."

"Me, neither."

She handed him a paper. "Please look this over critically, Casey. It's my report of Smitty's suicide. We'll need it for the ship's log as well as the authorities in Banda Aceh."

Casey raised an eyebrow at the word. "Suicide?"

She shrugged. "What else? No known witnesses. No evidence of homicide."

"Did you find time to check for fingerprints on those opened packages of fentanyl?"

"Lots of smudges," she acknowledged. "Smitty's were the only clear prints."

Casey stood and stretched. "What little evidence we have certainly supports your report. But…"

She moistened her lips. "What?"

He let his breath out. "I don't think Smitty broke into the sick bay and stole those drugs. I bet our unknown killer did.

"Smitty was handed the drugs, someone--maybe our murderer--claimed they were sleep aids. So Smitty went to the toilet, swallowed a few and BANG!"

He clapped his hands for emphasis. "He's dead!"

She jumped at the loud noise. "Then perhaps I should write 'Person or persons unknown stole the drugs and made them available to the deceased.' How's that?"

"Don't let me influence your professional opinion."

Uncomfortable, she asked, "Think we could put Smitty's body in our walk-in frig until we dock?"

"Sure, Kathlee. Let's hope there are no more bodies seeking similar accommodations."

A small, flickering fluorescent tube lighted the only way down the companionway to the engine room and pump station. Once below, overhead lights brightly illuminated the throbbing hulks of dark machinery propelling the twelve-year-old oil tanker hrough the Andaman Sea.

"The lighting down here once made an old visitor describe the dark, forbidding hold of the *Mayaguez*," Casey chuckled.

"He said, 'It's like descending into hell!"

The heavy, monotonous purr of the diesels, the pulsing of the generators and pumps combined into a crescendo which would have heightened that visitor's illusion.

Franz Suppe, Second Engineer, slouched in a deck chair watching the control console. Occasionally, he picked up a pencil and recorded numbers and pressure levels in the engineering daily log.

Beyond the console, Cruz, the surviving new replacement, carried an old-fashioned squirt can, oiling connections.

Cruz paused, calling back to Suppe, "Did you see Smitty's body in the can?"

Suppe flipped to a fresh page in the log. "No, I didn't."

He added as an afterthought, "Hell of a place to die. All alone and sitting on the throne."

"Yeah. Terrible."

"You were there, right?" Suppe asked. "You saw him go into the head with those pills or whatever they were?"

"Yeah, but don't say anything. I told the Security Officer and Captain that I didn't see or know anything."

"What else did they ask you?"

"They asked where the pills came from. Told them I didn't know that, either. We all did."

Still in the deck chair, Suppe stretched. "Well, someone stole them outa' the sick bay. Knocked open that glass medicine chest in there, I heard."

Cruz raised his head from squirting a connection with oil. "No, they wanted to know how Smitty got them, not where they came from. Again, we all said we didn't know."

Suppe smirked. "Bet I'm the only one who knows that."

Cruz wiped oil from his arm with cotton waste. "You know how Smitty got those pills? Tell me," he whispered.

Immediately, Suppe backtracked. "I mean, indirectly, I know."

"Well?"

"After we unloaded in George Town, I noticed a little package in the scupper on main deck. I bet it contained those pills, or whatever they were. You or one of your buddies must have picked it out of the scupper."

Kathlee stared at her face in the mirror over the wash basin. "We must find our killer before we make that next delivery at Nancowry…"

He finished her sentence. "Or we won't have a crew left aboard the *Bangor* to operate, maintain or unload cargo. We will be dead in the water," he scowled.

"I still think there's something very valuable aboard this ship that we don't know about. That's what provides the killer a motive to take over the ship."

Kathlee held up a hand. "We even went through the manifest, looking for something valuable enough to kill off our crew…"

"You and I included." Casey added.

"Still carry that pistol?" he asked, staring at her dungarees and jacket.

She patted a hidden ankle holster. "Right here. Let's review the suspects again. Maybe something will pop-up that we've overlooked.

"First suspect is always the First Mate," she rubbed her forehead. "What about Avery?"

"May I bum a cigarette"

"Sure. Light me one, too."

He stood close, watching her expression as he passed her a lighted cigarette. "He claimed that Park was the murderer, based on his drinking habit."

"He was angry at Park because he had to bail him out of jail in Grenada. That was a long time ago."

"Scratch the First Mate from suspicion? What about Tejada?

She sat on one side of her bunk. "You called the hiring hall in George Town. They said they hadn't seen Tejada. Why did he lie about looking for replacements?"

"I've no idea yet," Casey rubbed his unshaven chin. "He's a prime suspect."

Kathlee leaned forward to touch his chin. "Let's eliminate Cruz, the replacement. He's brand new."

Casey held his breath following her touch. Breathing again, he questioned, "Friauf and Suppe? One of them could have been on deck stalking Saldana or Smitty, the other one working below."

"Papa Alonzo," she continued. "We can eliminate the cook, can't we? He's not strong enough to heave Saldana's body overboard."

He chuckled. "I remember you saying those same words your first day aboard."

"Am I still on your suspect list, Captain Flynn?"

He shook his head. "Not since you let me into your cabin without a qualm…or a pistol."

Ignoring his look, she clasped her hands. "That leaves Park and Partagas, among others. Any suspicions about those two?"

"Fine sleuths we are," he exhaled. "We need evidence, not suspicions."

Kathlee counted on her fingers. "That's everyone except…"

He sat up. "Except who?"

Suddenly the hallway squawk box sounded. "Captain to the bridge!"

CHAPTER FOURTEEN

"TROUBLE?" SHE ANSWERED his special knock an hour later, loosely holding her Glock pisol.

He shook his head, "We coming into Nancowry shortly. It should be a quick discharge since the port capacity is small compared to our other customers. Besides, we can't grant shore leave here because we are so short-handed. Luckily, Nancowry is not popular among our crew, or so the First Mate tells me.

"I'm pleased you answered the door with a pistol handy."

"I still have to go ashore to report Smitty's death to the police. I'll also make arrangements for his body..."

He interrupted. "Sorry I didn't tell you earlier. We received a message from Smitty's family in Utah. They want his remains shipped to them from Port Blair. We'll have to keep him refrigerated in the locker for a bit longer.

"Who's going to accompany you ashore?"

She pursed her lips. "You're most welcome to come. We might even have a quick drink ashore somewhere."

He bit his lip, staring at hers. "Wish I could, but I've got to stay on board during the hasty unloading. The fastest discharges are the most dangerous. Sorry," he finished lamely.

"I undertstand completely. Guess Tejada will go to the police with me since he knows the way. I'll stay safe, don't worry!

"Speaking of Tejada, did you question him about his absence at that hiring hall?"

"Sorry," he lamented. "Should have, but didn't get the chance alone with him. I did, however, check the engine room log sheets on the dates of the three deaths."

"Murders," she corrected.

"Murders," he agreed. "Friauf and Suppe usually split the midnight shift. I can't be certain which one was on duty during those particular hours. While you're gone, I intend to individually grill Partagas and Park about Smitty. They were both on duty that night."

"Be careful, Casey"

"Don't forget our signal. Dum, de, dum dum."

She roused Casey the next morning by wafting a carafe of coffee under his nose. He struggled to sit up while holding the blanket.

"You always sleep commando?"

Opening his eyes, he nodded while sipping coffee. "Don't tell your father," he joked.

"I'm sure he would not approve his daughter bringing me coffee in bed, much less ogling a nude male."

Playfully, she tugged the blanket. "I'll ask when I talk to him today."

"My God! You've been giving him daily reports on our troubles here?"

She ignored the question. "Back to basics, what happened during your patrolling last night?"

He rubbed his stubble. "All quiet. I talked to Partagas and Park about Smitty. Neither wanted to talk but Park let it slip that he really didn't know who brought that fentanyl into the sleeping bay."

His tone deepened. "As before, Kathlee, I'd appreciate you not going out on the deck alone, especially at night without your Glock companion," he frowned.

"Last night I had the eerie feeling that someone--other than Partagas and Park--was out there watching me."

"But you saw no one?"

"Correct, I saw no one. I even hid in a dark corner a couple of times, but no luck. I had a definite feeling that I wasn't alone out there."

After breakfast in the mess with a sullen but silent crew. Kathlee waited until the last crewman left. "I have another plan," she said softly.

"Tonight I'll be on the bridge by twenty-three hundred hours. You signal me whenever you feel there's someone out there with you.

"I'll immediately turn on the deck lights. You identify who it is and we corral him."

Breathless, she added, "We'll finally have our killer!"

"Maybe worth a try," Casey conceded "What else do we have? But remember, I want you to have that pistol in hand anytime you're out of your cabin."

The noisy whirl of the potato peelers carried all the way to the bridge, Alonzo knew. He emptied one machine of skinned spuds and refilled it.

To most of the crew, galley sounds were bothersome. To Alonzo, they were music, a familiar tune evoking memories of summertime and promenading around the village square. Males always walked in one direction, he smiled at the thought, and females in the opposite.

Suddenly, both potato peelers stalled, their chatter stilled. The kitchen, Alonzo's private musical domain, was silent.

In the sudden quiet he could hear muted voices from inside the mess. Two men were talking.

Puzzled, he cracked open the small serving window

between the mess and galley. Why would anyone whisper in his mess? He edged closer to the serving window.

"We're behind on the schedule sent us," one voice, rising in irritation, complained. "We still have seven dummies left on board. This plan says there should only be five guys by now."

"Not my fault," the other voice rose in defense. "That captain arrives at all hours to disrupt things."

"Eliminate the negative, as the saying goes."

"I'll need your help."

"Make a plan this time and we'll do it."

Alonzo backed away from the serving window. He didn't need look to identify the two men. If he looked out, they might see him.

Then their plan would include eliminating him if they knew he overheard. Holding his breath, he backed toward the stove.

As quickly as it had ceased, the electric power resumed and the potato peelers hummed again. Crouched behind the big black stove, Alonzo crossed himself, only half-breathing until the two men were gone.

Although she spoofed Casey about his warnings, Kathlee kept a hand near her pistol as she climbed up to the bridge.

Surprised by her sudden appearance, the First Mate and Tejada quit their relaxed conversation beside the console to stare.

She pulled up a folding chair. "Good evening, gentlemen. I thought I'd join you. Everything all right?" She reached for the ever-present coffee pot and poured herself a cup.

"All quiet, ma'm," Tejada replied. The First Mate merely nodded before transferring his attention back to his charts.

"We're making good progress. Seas are calm," Tejada indicated their position on the big map.

Eyes on the map, she shifted her chair closer to the panel switches and adjusted the I-phone in her lap.

There was a click from her I-phone and she leaned forward to switch on all the deck lights.

The First Mate bristled. "Why did you do that? Now we're blind as bats up here until our night vision is restored."

"Sorry if I startled you, First Mate," she apologized with a smile.

"I was **not** startled," he retorted. "As First Mate, I should be told in advance what sudden changes you're about to make to our routine. Does the Captain know what you're doing?"

Kathlee ignored both the hostility and question. "We'll dock sometime in the morning, right?"

Grinning at the tension between the two, Tejada answered again. "Our ETA is about eleven hundred hours,"

Lighting a cigarette, the First Mate tried regain his aplomb. "Add five hours to that for hosing and unloading," he nodded through the smoke.

"So we'll be ready to shove off for Port Blair by sixteen hundred. Hope you and the Captain can be back by then," he added cryptically.

Eyes snapping, she dared him. "You'd leave us behind, First Mate?"

"I'd surely hate that, ma'm," he began, "but…"

A cry from behind them erased Avery's smirk.

Kathlee upended her chair, "What's that?"

Outside on the companionway, they joined several crewmen. Wordless, the sailors parted for them and pointed.

Within their small circle a body lay crumpled on the stairs beside the mess entrance.

"Cruz," she sighed as she turned him over and leaned down, searching for a pulse. Finding none, she placed her ear on his chest, hoping for a heart beat.

Sitting up, shaking her head, she noticed blood covering both her hands. Then she examined the back of his head.

"He's dead!"

She spat at the shocked faces surrounding her. "Who did this?

"Who did this? One of you did!"

Amid the ringing chorus of 'Not me, not me' Casey stormed down from the bridge. He pushed aside Park and Suppe to stare at Kathlee, kneeling beside the still body of Cruz.

"Oh, Lord! Not another one!"

Her bloody hands trembling, she wiped them on her shirt. "Yes, Captain. This time it's Cruz."

"Inside the mess, everyone," Casey ordered. "We'll sort this out right now," he lifted an ashen Kathlee to her feet.

"We can't leave his body out here," the just-arrived First Mate objected.

Recovering quickly, Kathlee directed, "Assign a man to remain here with Cruz until we've finished inside. Who will it be?"

Avery nodded at the closest man. "Park, you stay here with him."

"Don't move or touch anything!" Casey warned as he held the mess door open. "Everybody into the mess!"

Inside, he walked about, pointing places he wanted them to occupy. "Sit apart, men. No talking."

"Alonzo, you're first." She took the cook by the arm and sat him in the adjoining day room across from Casey and herself.

"What were you doing at…" she checked her watch, "at twenty-three forty-five?"

Wiping his hands on a once-white apron, Alonzo fidgeted. "I had just starting serving supper to the midnight shift."

The sight of Alonzo's hands made her stop. "Captain, we should immediately check everyone's hands for traces of blood."

Casey nodded and, crossing the hall, started examining outstretched hands, palms and arms.

Kathlee continued with Alonzo. "Who did you serve in the mess?"

"The midnight shift, Miss."

"Names, Alonzo. Names."

"Well...Park, Partagas, eh..."

"Who else?"

Alonzo made a cathedral with his fingers. "Houser, I think was already there. Suppe came in through the door when Houser spilled coffee all over the table and I had to clean it up."

Casey entered, shaking his head about not finding any traces of blood on the crew. He patted Alonzo's shoulder in encouragement.

"How long were you in the galley and out of the mess?"

Alonzo scratched his pate. "Just a few minutes, I think."

"When you retuned to the mess, who had entered while you were in the galley?"

Alonzo wiped his forehead with an edge of the apron. "I dunno. By then I was busy serving the beans and franks."

"Did you see Cruz in the mess or on the stairs?"

"No, Miss."

"Thank you. You may go back to your work now. Don't talk to anyone about Cruz, Okay?"

Partagas and Houser were interviewed separately but their statements coincided.

Both claimed to be entering the mess when they heard someone tumble in the companionway below. Neither saw Cruz fall. Both claimed they saw no one else nearby.

Agreeing to Casey's instruction not to discuss Cruz, they returned to the mess.

"Get back to me and the security officer if you think of anything else," he said as they departed the day room.

Second Engineer Suppe said he and Cruz were below in

the engine room. Suppe left early for the mess because he was hungry. He said he presumed Cruz would follow him in a few minutes.

"Did you see Cruz in the companionway, following you to the mess?"

"No, sir."

"Did you hear him fall?"

Suppe shook his head.

"What was Cruz' demeanor, Mr. Suppe?"

"How's that?"

"Was Cruz nervous or anxious about anything? Did he appear worried or afraid?"

"He seemed normal to me, Captain."

As Casey and Kathlee finished with each man, he returned to supper.

The normally noisy mess table was silent for a change. Each man sat glumly chewing and leaving the table as soon as he could.

Houser rose to leave at the end of his interview. Kathlee asked him to replace Park, standing outside with Cruz' body, and to send Park inside for questioning.

Park remembered hearing someone--he guessed Cruz-- climbing the stairs behind him. "But I had not seen Cruz since noon," he insisted.

Park cleared his throat. "May I ask a question?"

"Of course."

"Who's the next one to be killed on this bloody ship?"

CHAPTER FIFTEEN

AFTER PHOTOGRAPHING THE scene and Cruz' body, Kathlee dusted the hallway handrails for prints but found only smudges.

"No weapon?"

"No, Casey. From the terrible fracture on the back of his head, I'd say it was a metal pipe or truncheon."

"Or a police baton like we arm the deck guards at night?"

"I checked our batons already," she sat on her bunk, sipping the coffee Casey had just handed her.

"The pipe, or whatever, probably was thrown overboard."

"Very likely."

Casey looked doubtful. "I'd better check the decks anyway. What do we do about the body?"

She brushed auburn hair from her forehead with a hand. "I'll have him put in the sick bay where I can examine him thoroughly."

"I'll do that," he volunteered. "The crew is rattled enough and I can do that by myself."

Once they reached the sick bay, she held open the splintered door for Casey to enter with his burden.

In an hour, she was finished. Washing-up, she asked Casey to move the body to the walk-in refrigerator in the galley.

Later they returned to Kathlee's cabin and sat down, discouraged. With a grin, she held up a bottle of cognac.

"I think we need a little restorative, Captain." She half-filled two glasses.

"Cheers!"

"Cheers," he repeated, admiring her ability to recover.

They studied each other before she set down her empty glass.

"Was Tejada with you on the bridge when you heard the shout about Cruz?"

"Yes. Karl Friauf was below, tending the diesels by himself, he said."

Casey checked his notepad. "According to Alonzo, Park, Partagas and Houser were in the mess. Suppe, coming through the door, thought Cruz was somewhere behind him. He claimed he did not actually see Cruz on the stairs."

"Any ideas, Casey?" she pleaded.

"We've go to stop this slaughter! We barely have enough crew to sail the *Bangor* to our next delivery port."

He returned to his notes. "The only people not inside or entering the mess were Tejada on the bridge and Friauf in the engine room."

"They seem our best suspects, don't you think? Tejada and Friauf." With that, she half-filled their glasses again.

"You'd better alert the port police at Port Blair that some of our crew are likely to jump ship there. Naturally, they are traumatized by these unsolved murders."

"We're all that way, including the two of us."

Looking grim, Casey added, "Except for the murderer or murderers. Before Cruz' death, when you turned on the deck lights, did you see anyone?"

"Only shadows," she responded. "Did you still have that gut feeling that you were being watched by someone out there?"

"Definitely. Well…" he scratched his head, "let's hope for an uneventful cargo discharge at Port Blair this morning. I'm going below to question Friauf again, then back to the bridge.

"I see your pistol is still there," he patted her.

"Yes, the Glock is still there, Casey.

"But **not** where you patted."

Overlooking the Duncan Passage, Port Blair glistened from the intensity of the rising sun. New buildings seemed to teeter on the edges of the coastline, each competing for scarce space near the Passage.

Not far from the new port facilities being constructed near the *Bangor's* anchorage, several small hotels and resorts sprouted like seedlings encouraged by the bright sun.

Kathlee and Casey watched their crew perform the rituals of attaching long hoses to the shore pier, checking hose pressures, then beginning the off-loading of oil from tank number one.

Casey pointed to several uniformed policemen who paced the pier area. "Congratulations on their presence, Kathlee. Happily, they probably already associate you with your famous father."

"Happy? No. The police chief was quite unhappy when I handed him my report on the Cruz death. He asked how many seamen have we lost on this trip? I told him and he quickly wished us a 'bon voyage' out of his port as soon as possible."

Casey touched the auburn curls escaping from under her woolen cap. "We always seem to be in a hurry, don't we?"

"Meaning what?"

"You've been secretive about your life, ambitions, pleasures, regrets. I'd like to know more about my new Security Officer. I don't even know--here's an easy one--were you born in Bridgetown?"

"Yes," she stepped back. "I told you already."

He moved down the railing, in step with her. "Brothers? Sisters? Happy childhood? Favorite color? Have a pet at home?"

She fumed. "As I told you before: no brothers or sisters. If you find me demanding, it's because I grew up among a tribe of cantankerous males led by my father.

"Mother died when I was three, and…"

"Sorry," he interrupted. "Didn't mean to intrude and I'm doing exactly that."

She backed off again. "But you're still curious, aren't you, about the capricious female for whom you are now responsible to her father, the CEO of *Seatrans*."

"Yes. More curious than ever. What about schooling? London School of Economics?"

"University of the West Indies. Don't you listen? I told you that before, too.

"Whoa! That's enough!"

To divert his attention, she motioned to the deck crew working below. "Those guys are terribly overworked, you know. We've found no volunteers willing to sign up to work on your infamous ship.

"Look!" she pointed. "There's the reason."

On the pier, a black funeral hearse was being loaded with Cruz' body. Everyone on deck stopped work to somberly watch the coffin being loaded. Slowly, the hearse pulled away. The crew stared after it for long minutes.

"Back to work!" shouted the First Mate.

CHAPTER SIXTEEN

O N THEIR WAY to the bridge, Kathlee touched his arm. "I have another idea."

"Let's hear it"

"Let's ask Avery, Tejada, Friauf and Suppe to move from their cabins into the crew sleeping bay. That way we have all our men in one place.

"Easier to account for *and* easier to safeguard!"

Casey liked it. "Everyone keeps an eye on everyone else. Great!"

"Exactly," she grinned. "Hopefully, further mayhem may be less likely."

Casey stopped in the companionway. "But that sounds like putting the cat in the canary cage. I think at least one of that foursome must be our murderer or know who the murderer is."

"All right," she stopped him with a hand on his chest. "Here's another idea. Starting now we split up. You take the two men in the engine room and I shadow the two on the bridge."

"Definitely not!" He touched her hand. "Too dangerous. I'm not letting you, 'capricious female,' out of my sight."

She pulled open the door to the bridge before he could reach it. "We'll discuss this later, in private."

They later retreated to Kathlee's cabin for a serious conference. "What'll we do now, Casey?"

"Let's discontinue the two-man deck patrol at night. We

simply don't have the manpower. I walk the main deck alone.
You, in the bridge, wait for my signal to turn on the deck lights
if I sense--or see--someone out there with me."

She frowned. "If the killer knows there is no two-man
patrol on the deck, you're his only target."

Hands on hips, she accused him. "You nixed my idea
because of danger to me."

She turned both thumbs down in his face. "I don't like
your idea for the same reason!"

"Did you forget?" He patted the pistol on his hip. "I'm well
protected out there."

She changed their mood by brandishing cognac and
glasses. Nodding, they took their usual opposing chairs.

She raised her glass. "Cheers! Let's declare a temporary
truce."

He repeated the toast, grinning. "We'll see."

"We begin our truce," she announced, "with your telling
a bit about yourself. These questions are identical to the ones
you asked me, so they must be important.

"Brothers and sisters?"

"Kathlee! Must we do this so late at night? You are
exhausted."

"Answer the questions, Casey. Then you're free to conduct
your deck patrol."

Exasperated, Casey agreed. "Just a few questions, okay?

"I have a brother in the Naval Academy and a sister in
Phoenix. Parents both deceased."

"Favorite color?"

Arms folded, he shook his head. "I asked you that same
question and you never answered."

"I'm answering now. Blue. You?"

"Tangerine."

She stood face to face. "If you're going to be comical, forget it. Go on your deck inspection but don't expect hot coffee from me in the morning."

He took her by the arm. "Not happy with my answers? How about we go to supper now?"

The midnight shift gathering in the mess for supper numbered only four crewmen. The four, Avery, Tejada, Friauf and Suppe, outnumbered Casey, Kathlee and Alonzo, seated across the table from them.

Casey left the table to begin patrolling the main deck.

At 0200 hours Casey stood, admiring the buttery half moon hanging over the starboard quarter. The Andaman Sea was placid for the moment. Only a few rolling waves wrinkled the moonlit watery carpeting.

Despite the absence of a third of its normal crew, the *Bangor* made good headway toward its next port of call, Great Coco Island.

The only light came from the bridge's front window far above Casey, looking like the eye of a huge Cyclops.

He leaned on the rail, momentarily picturing Kathlee standing on the bridge, awaiting his signal to turn on the deck lights.

"Unusual lady," he said aloud, turning around to assure he was alone. "She's a bit of a scrapper, certainly not the regular rich man's spoiled little daughter."

"I admire that!" he shot a fist into the air.

At that moment he thought he saw a shadow move beside the port ventilator. He moved to investigate, pistol in hand.

Thanking her for the hot cup of coffee brought to awaken him, Casey rolled over and sipped the hot brew.

"Last night you said I would be denied hot coffee this morning."

"I relented," she said. "Get dressed so I can ask you more questions."

Leaving his cabin door ajar, Kathee sipped her own coffee in the hall while Casey dressed inside.

They headed for breakfast in the mess. "Nothing to report," he began their usual exchange. "I thought I saw someone but it was just a shadow.

"Even the crew sleeping bay was quiet, despite their probable many bad dreams."

She held out her plate for the fried eggs, bread and cheese being served cafeteria style by Alonzo.

"Have some more," Alonzo urged. "We've got plenty of food since the crew is so small."

Casey filled two cups from the coffee machine and sat down beside Kathlee and several crewmen.

"How are you doing, Park?" he asked the man beside him.

Park yawned and shook his head. "I'm tired, Captain. Mighty hard to sleep good when you know someone is likely to be knocked-off or disappear. Maybe it will be me, you can't help but think."

"Yeah," Partagas agreed. "It's like swimming alongside a great white shark. You don't know when he'll turn and gobble you. But you know he will."

Avery and Friauf sat at the next table, smoking and drinking coffee. Silently, they shot angry glances at Partagas.

Casey turned toward them. "Where's Tejada this morning?"

Blinking, Avery replied. "He was on duty all night again. Surprised you didn't see him during your rounds on deck.

"I just relieved him a bit ago. He's probably bunked-out and dead to the world at the moment. Are you sending him ashore on Great Coco to find us some replacements?"

"Absolutely. I hope he'll have more success than earlier. God knows, we need help."

Casey noticed with surprise that Kathlee crossed herself on hearing his words.

That evening Casey and Kathlee agreed to keep joint watch on the deck, although Casey's agreement was guarded.

"I think you deserve a quick walk around the deck with me. That ought to restore that optimistic attitude of yours which I've been admiring."

"I'm thankful for your advice and support on this murderous voyage," she began.

"Thankful enough to tell your father he made the right decision by giving my first command?"

She huffed. "Don't be facetious, Casey. I wouldn't be here if I thought you weren't the man for this job."

He looked at her for a long moment, before suggesting they go to supper.

"You go to supper first, Casey. Later you spell me and we'll take that walk around the deck you suggested."

After supper, they locked her cabin door and went below to the main deck. The moon highlighted everything on deck including the man and woman standing closely beside the rail, watching the sea.

"Think this voyage will ever end, Casey?"

"Of course it will. Successful, too! Where's that optimism?"

Not only had her cheerful mood diminished, she was exhausted. He helped her unsteadily to her cabin. Once here, Casey removed her heavy shoes and tucked her into bunk and blankets.

He moistened a cloth and placed it on her forehead. Filling a glass with water, he took several aspirin from a bottle on her washstand.

"Open up," he motioned. "These might make you feel a bit better."

She sat up, removing the cold cloth from her face. "Thanks, Casey. I'm all right now."

She downed the aspirin and water. "Guess I was tired. Sorry for your trouble."

She looked at him for a reaction. "On a domestic note, I gathered up your dirty clothes from those piles on the floor of your cabin and washed them."

"Obviously, you shouldn't have, Security Officer. I thank you very much."

To relieve his embarrassment, he grabbed a blank paper from her desk and began writing. "I'll be right back."

Moments later, he returned and sat on the bunk beside her. "Fed-up hearing all my unsuccessful plans?"

"No, Casey. I'm fine now.

"Remember, I'm Kathlee Sigmund, security officer and my father's strong and independent daughter!"

"Dum, de, dum, dum," Casey tapped on her door at 0100 hours. He carefully balanced two meal trays on one arm while knocking with the other hand.

She stepped aside. "Food! Oh, no!"

"An early breakfast for you, 'strong and independent daughter." He set the trays on her desk.

"Hungry? You should eat some of this." He sat and began eating.

"Nothing for me but the coffee, if it's still hot." She leaned back in her chair. "Have you changed your mind about our most likely suspects?"

He pushed aside the tray to face her. "Friauf and Tejada are still on my mind. Both were on the midnight shift."

"What about the men in the sleeping bay?"

"Surprisingly quiet. Only Park and Houser were there, apparently sleeping soundly."

"Suppe?"

"He just came off duty on the bridge."

To herself, she muttered, "Fine detectives! We still don't have a clue or motive!"

With that, she arose, stretched and pointed at the trays. "You planning to eat both those breakfasts?"

Comically, he smacked his lips. "Sure. Alonzo will be insulted if I returned them untouched. While I'm returning the trays and starting my deck patrol, shouldn't you get some sleep?"

The sleeping bay Casey earlier described as quiet was a hubbub of noise and confusion the next morning. Partagas and Houser stood in front of their angry captain.

"Who drank this?" Casey held up an empty vodka bottle.

Partagas wiped his forehead with a sleeve. "The three of us, sir."

Hauser nodded.

Casey looked from one to the other. "Where did this bottle come from?"

Neither seaman replied.

"I repeat, where did you get this bottle?"

Partagas looked at Houser, slowly nodding assent.

"Park said he found it under his pillow when we came off shift, sir."

"Then what happened?"

"The three of us sat on the stern and drank it."

"All of it?"

"Well, Captain," hoping for a reprieve, Houser emphasized the title. "Park drank most of it since he found it. It was rightfully his, sir.

"Partagas and I only had a swig or two, before Park grabbed it back and drank it down."

"You both broke regulations by drinking alcohol aboard ship. You are both in big trouble."

"Yes, sir," they said in unison.

"Then what happened?"

Partagas stammered. "Hard to explain or understand exactly, sir. It doesn't make sense…"

Houser finished the explanation. "Park pointed at the lights ashore over there," Houser nodded at an small island to the west.

"He said, 'I'm getting off this damned 'murder ship' and swimming ashore. I'll be much safer there than here."

Excitedly, Partagas resumed the story. "Park said he'd been told he was the leading name on that murder pool you abolished. He really was afraid he was the next to die!

"I can't believe what he did next!" Partagas shook his head.

Not to be denied, Houser cried, "Nor can I!

"He jumped off the port bulwark and started swimming toward the lights on that island over there."

Casey looked up from the notes he was taking. "You're lying! When Park took the bottle, you two struggled for it and threw him overboard!"

"No, Captain!" they both shouted. "We didn't touch him!"

Casey looked toward the nearest island. "That must be at least three or four miles away! Could you see him swimming for it after you threw him overboard?"

"No, sir," they both responded. "It was too dark. But we didn't throw him overboard, Captain! You've got to believe us!"

Casey checked his watch. "When did this happen?"

Agitated, Houser and Partagas looked at each other for the answer.

"Maybe three hours ago, Captain," Houser finally replied and Partagas nodded agreement.

Casey shook his fist at the two. "Why the hell didn't you give the alarm when he went overboard…unless you two threw him!

"By now he's either there or drowned. Too late to turn around and search for him in this dark," Casey decided.

To himself, Casey murmured. "Lots of sharks in this area. I'm afraid he never made it."

"Partagas," Casey pointed his finger. "get the Security Officer and First Mate and bring them here on the double. You and Houser are going to repeat your story to them.

"You better hope and pray that at least one of us believes your story!"

CHAPTER SEVENTEEN

SHE IGNORED HER bunk, instead showered, brushed her hair and selected what she thought was the most female of her few clothes.

> *Am I dressing up for the police at Great Coco*
> *or for Casey Flynn?*

A knock on the door interrupted her reverie. Pistol in hand, she opened the door a crack

A trembling Partagas stood there, wool cap in hand. "Captain says for you to come right away, Miss! And bring the First Mate, too."

Hearing real fright in his voice, Kathlee quickly joined him after locking her door. "What happened?"

Partagas shook his head. "Park got drunk and jumped overboard last night. I'm scared he drowned or the sharks got him, ma'm."

"Oh, no!"

"And the Captain thinks we pushed him. We didn't but I'm scared to death!"

"Where is the Captain?"

"On the main deck, ma'm, on the port rail near the bridge."

"Okay, I'm going there. You bring the First Mate. Got it?"

Minutes later, she and Casey sat in the mess, taking statements from Partagas and Houser.

"Do you really believe Park jumped overboard and tried to swim ashore?" She looked at Casey, then at the First Mate seated across from her.

"Never seen nobody that drunk," Avery muttered.

Alonzo was serving them coffee after statements were completed and Park and Houser dismissed to quarters.

"Think you can lift any prints off that vodka bottle?"

Kathlee bobbed her head. "Sure, I can. But they're likely to be smudges if all three handled the bottle.

"The question is," she reached for a coffee refill, "who provided the bottle? Did someone really place it under Park's pillow?

"The murderer?"

First Mate Avery agreed. "Must have been the murderer. But didn't we eliminate that 'murder pool' days ago?"

Glumly, Casey nodded. "We thought we did. Maybe the killer combined Park's known weakness for alcohol and his being told he was the pool's next victim?"

"Do we believe that Park jumped overboard or was thrown? Partagas and Houser are the only witnesses. They provide our only evidence."

Kathlee frowned, pursing her lips as Casey spoke. She had forgotten the lipstick in her rush to get there.

Now she had another chore, a report to prepare on Parks death.

"Should I call it a suicide on my report?"

Casey and Avery looked at each other, nodding grimly.

"Until we know more, what else can we say? I really doubt that Houser and Partagas heaved their shipmate over the rail."

She nudged Casey. "What about your nightly patrol, Captain? See anything of Park or the other two?"

"Only person I saw was Alonzo at 0400 this morning. He'd come by to pick up those breakfast trays I'd forgotten to return."

She studied him as he gathered up the statements from the

mess table. "Let's go to my cabin, Captain, so I can transmit these statements to my father's security team." They left the First Mate sitting there.

Once in her cabin, Casey said "I'd like us to review these new statements before we dock at Great Coco."

She winked. "Maybe a small cognac would expedite our review?"

He gave her a thumbs-up after checking that the passageway was vacant.

"Nervous to be in here alone with me, Captain?"

"No," he protested. "But what happened to 'good ole Casey'? Where did he go?"

They spent the early evening re-examining motives and suspects until they both were hazy. Nonetheless, Casey tried again, "If we knew the motive, we could identify the killer or killers. Right?

"There must be something aboard the *Bangor* motivating these murders or disappearances. First was Creech, then Saldana, Smitty, Cruz and now Park. Is there a commonality among them we don't understand?"

Kathlee poured them another half-drink. "Are you still convinced that Park was murdered? He may have been so inebriated that he fell overboard, despite what his two buddies say."

Casey ran his fingers through his beard. "I think the killer is outsmarting us at every move. He raised Park's apprehension by lying to him that he was next on that murder pool."

"How gullible! We announced the pool was abolished, gone for good."

Casey nodded but continued. "Nonetheless, a drunken Park thought his life was endangered. He thought he had to leave the ship by any means or be killed on it. I guess swimming away to any safe place sounded like survival to his addled brain.

"The murderer provided the death pool motivation. the bottle of vodka, then a means of escape, suggesting Park jump overboard and swim to safety."

She strongly disagreed. "I cannot believe any rational adult--even a drunken one--would think he could jump into the sea at night, swim several miles to an island, and survive."

Casey studied her. "That's a good point, Kathlee, several of them, in fact.

"By the way, you also broke company regulations about bringing alcohol," he lifted his glass in salute, "onboard."

"Guilty," she admitted. "Were it not for my cognac, you might have jumped overboard yourself."

She blinked her eyes, "Or had you another reason for staying?"

Case stood to stretch and evade her question. He patted her cheek. "Back to our problem, Madame Security Officer. Why is someone decimating our crew unless he or they intend to ultimately control this ship and gain whatever is in it?"

"Drugs, diamonds, gold? I didn't see any of those on the manifest," she spoofed.

Casey stretched again. "I have another plan," he whispered.

"Tell me."

"I'm going to be the irresistible bait this time!"

CHAPTER EIGHTEEN

LOW HILLS. DENSE with exotic trees, interspersed by a few small houses, overlooked the *Bangor's* anchorage. Despite its name, Great Coco was a small island, populated by only a few dozen inhabitants. Like people everywhere, they required petroleum products. The arrival of the oil tanker always caused a happy gathering of residents along the lone pier.

The highlight of their year was a week-long merriment and music-filled carnival imitating the huge one taking place in Rangoon on the mainland.

Today, as the *Bangor* nudged the pier's bollards, Kathlee likened Great Coco to a colorful postcard scene as she looked out her porthole.

She awakened Casey with the usual cup of coffee delivered to his cabin.

To assure he was awake, she asked, "Any visitors last night during your vigil?"

"Thanks for the coffee, Kathlee. No, no visitors."

He exhaled heavily. "My ruse to lure the killer to get at me failed. So far, he or them, are too clever for me."

She pointed out his porthole. "We're at the pier, hooking up and will start discharging oil soon. I plan to go ashore with Second Mate Tejada and again attempt to recruit us some warm bodies."

Casey ran a hand through rumpled hair. "Please be careful

ashore. I'm sure your lovely presence will mesmerize several recruits."

He studied her new hair-do and lacquered nails. "You'll also be busy with the police, reporting Park's disappearance and presumed suicide?"

At her nod, he winkled his nose. "All I'm doing ashore is buying a door to replace the one damaged in the sick bay. Don't be disappointed if no one wants to sign-on our 'murder ship' despite that engaging manner of yours."

On his return from Coco's small business district, Casey joined the deck crew checking the heavy discharge lines. When the discharge of oil tank four began, he turned to watch the transfer of shrimp containers into vacant deck space.

He nodded to Alonzo lugging boxes to and from the cargo nets. "Good work, Papa!"

Alonzo's chest and fat stomach bobbed. "We're so short of crew, sir.

"And look at those policemen over there, watching us. Why are they on the pier?"

Casey answered with a shrug. "Looking for contraband, I guess."

He heard a shout, "Captain to the bridge." Answering with a wave of his hand, he began climbing up the ladder. Not knowing who was killing the crewmen on his own ship--his first command--always doubled his angst as he entered the bridge.

He caught his breath. Below him, on the pier, Kathlee marched toward the *Bangor*. Canvas bag slung over her shoulder, she strode past the smiling policemen and up the ship's rolling gangway.

"I'm responsible for the safety of everyone here, including her," he ground his teeth. "I'm failing all of them!"

On the main deck she stopped short, waved at him, and pantomimed there were no recruits. Suddenly, she grabbed her

I-phone, halting for a long conversation. From her expression, Casey knew it was bad news.

Once aboard, almost tearing, she admitted, "It was my father. C'mon. Let's go to my cabin and I'll tell you what he said."

Inside, they sat down in their usual places. She rubbed her forehead as a prelude to telling him the news, wondering if it would please or depress him.

"Dad wants me to fly home. He says I'm in danger here and wants me off the ship immediately. He even booked me a flight out of Rangoon tomorrow morning!"

She waited for Casey's strong, she hoped, reaction.

Exhaling, he shut his eyes.

"I admire your father," Casey spoke slowly, deliberately. "He and I want the same thing, your safety."

Unhappy with his mild reaction, she added. "I told him our situation, we have barely enough men to sail and are unable to hire more."

She reached into the canvas shoulder bag at her feet. "My only good news is that I bought this after seeing the police."

With a flourish, she pulled out a new bottle of cognac and thumped it on the table.

He jumped up. "No time for that! We've got to pack you right away, get you to the mainland and to the airport for that flight. Give me your I-phone and I'll arrange us a helicopter if I can."

She whispered, "You said 'us,' Casey?"

"That's right. **Us.**"

She acted as if she were shocked. "You can't just leave your ship and crew! You're the captain!"

"Well," he patted her cheek. "**You** are as vital to this ship and crew as me! How could you possibly leave?"

She clapped her hands. "I love your choice of that 'Us'

word, Casey. I've already decided something about us, you, me, ship and crew."

She answered his raised eyebrows.

"We're in this together, Casey Flynn! I'm not leaving. To hell with my father!"

Once the ship cleared Great Coco and was underway for the last delivery to Preparis Island, Kathlee called her father with her decision to remain on the *Bangor*.

"Whew!" she winked at Casey. "He's mad as hell!"

He grinned. "Kathlee, don't worry! Once we eventually return to Barbados, I'll swear that I physically forced you to disobey him and stay aboard."

She winked. "There goes your promising maritime career, Captain. Did you see it just capsize?"

"Maybe not! You and I can start our own shipping company!"

CHAPTER NINETEEN

A TTENDANCE AT SUPPER that night again illustrated the diminishing size of the crew. Alonzo attempted to serve double portions of beans and rice to all his diners.

"We've got to eat it," he cajoled. "Can't throw it overboard for the sharks to eat."

"Sorry!" he realized his gaffe.

Tejada, just arrived from the bridge, accepted extra helpings. "I'm gaining weight," he joked, "to prepare for my Hollywood screen test next month."

The others sat, stoically regarding their plates, instead of each other.

Attempting to lighten the mood, Casey spoke to each man at the table. Partagas and Houser nodded at his attempts, but didn't reply.

Suddenly, Suppe rose and left for the engine room. Avery told everyone that he was turning-in for a few hours after an all-night duty and asked Tejada to return to the bridge later to substitute for him.

Motioning the captain outside, Kathlee tugged at his arm. "Casey, I want to speak to Houser and Partagas before they leave.

"They both look so miserable and despondent that I want to try to cheer them up, but not in front of the others."

"You're marvelous!" was his response. "You'll be a great

shipping company CEO: efficient, observant, plus you really care about people.

"Your concern about those two must mean you think the murderer is among the other five."

"Four, Casey. I don't think Alonzo is the killer, do you?"

Partagas was first out the door. "Got a minute, Pancho?" Casey took his elbow.

"We'd like a word with you. We know you're feeling anxious about those deaths," Kathlee began. "What can the Captain and I do to make you feel safer?"

Dumbfounded, Partagas looked from one to the other. "Well…uhh. Nice of you to take the time to talk to me."

He looked down the long corridor toward the crew quarters. "I can't think of anything right now. I've still got my knife with me, so I'm pretty safe." He raised his shirt to show them.

"I'll be all right. But I'm real worried about my buddy, Hoosier. He's acting mighty strange since Park jumped overboard."

"Strange? How? Give us an example?"

"Well, ma'm, he talks dopey at times. Has nightmares about Park. He told me Park even talks to him in his dreams.

"But don't tell him I told you! What do you think I can do to help him?"

"We'll talk to Hoosier right now, but won't tell what you said. Thanks, Pancho."

The mess door swung open again as Hoosier Houser came out. Partagas wandered away down the corridor.

"May we talk to you for a minute, Hoosier?"

"Yes, miss."

"We are all concerned about everyone's safety, just as you are. Any ideas how we can help you feel more secure?"

Houser cringed at the question as he stared down the darkened hallway.

"Have you been sleeping okay?"

He expelled his breath. "No, miss. Funny you ask 'cause I have trouble going to sleep sometimes. Too many bad things happening on this ship."

Casey pressed. "What is it that keeps you awake? Can you tell us?"

"Bad dreams mostly, sir. Last night I dreamed Park was sitting on the next bunk and talking to me."

They both leaned forward. "What did he say?"

Houser turned and lowered his voice. "Gary wants me to follow him to the 'safe place' as he calls it."

"Where is his safe place?"

Houser steadied himself with a hand against the bulkhead. "Clear as a bell, he said, 'Follow me and I'll show you!'"

Kathlee felt of Houser's wrist, taking his pulse. "I'll give you something to help you sleep better."

Later, in the sick bay, she watched Houser swallow a mild sedative. As he left, he clutched an envelope containing a few aspirin.

She turned to Casey once Houser left. "I'm really concerned about him. But what can I do?"

He patted her shoulder. "You've shown him more care and compassion than he's ever known. I bet he'll feel much better in the morning after a good night's rest.

"I'll check on him in a few hours as I patrol the deck."

"Thank you, Casey. You be careful out there, on deck by yourself."

As an aside, she whispered, "Still got your pistol?"

CHAPTER TWENTY

HEARING A SCREAM an hour later, Casey burst into the crew sleeping bay. Panting and trembling, Partagas stood in the middle of the room, shouting.

"It's a sign! A sign! Hoosier kept saying it!"

Houser's body hung limply from a rope over his bunk. The rope was attached to an overhead steam pipe.

Casey grabbed Hoosier's feet, trying to support his heavy body.

"Use your knife, Partagas! Cut the rope!" Casey shouted, trying to heist Houser's body upward to ease the tension on the rope.

Partagas hacked at the rope, finally separating it. Houser's entire weight made Casey stumble as the inert body slipped downward into his arms.

He managed to balance the body momentarily as he staggered with it toward Houser's bunk. The severed hangman's rope dangled above them.

"FETCH HER!" he commanded the trembling Partagas.

In a minute, Kathlee appeared with her medical kit. She blurted, "Partagas said there was an accident!" Then she saw the body in the bunk.

Casey moved aside so she could examine Houser. "He doesn't seem to be breathing.

"I was too late!" he lamented.

"Yes, too late," she whispered. "I'm too late, too. What happened?"

Casey shoved Partagas onto an empty bunk. "Take a deep breath and tell us what you saw and heard."

Head in hand, Partagas was sobbing softly. Casey draped an arm about the sobbing man. Kathlee handed him a tissue.

"Take your time, Pancho. What happened?"

He wiped his eyes and sat up. "That rope," he pointed at it.

"When Hoosier and I came back from talking to you outside the galley, that rope was there, swinging right above his bunk."

"Hoosier started yelling as soon as he saw it. 'A sign! A sign!

"I thought someone had hung it up as a joke to scare us while we were gone. But the bay was empty. No one was there except Hoosier and me.

"I started to stand on his bunk and cut it down. But Hoosier yelled, 'Don't touch it! It's for me!'"

Partagas covered his eyes. "I thought he meant he was going to take the rope down himself and didn't want me standing on his bunk.

"I had to go to the head, I was so scared. I was only gone for a minute. When I got back, he was hanging there, the rope around his neck. It was so tight he was turning purple, his tongue sticking out."

His sobbing resumed. "It was horrible! Horrible!"

Kathlee grabbed a shoulder. "We understand, Pancho. It was terrible and you've been very brave to tell us. I must write your words in a report later. I'll have to ask you to swear to and sign that report."

She helped Partagas to his feet. "Casey, I'm putting him in the sick bay for tonight. He can't stay here. I'll give him a strong sedative so he can sleep, maybe."

Casey nodded. "Good. I'll stay here 'til you return with your camera."

She was back shortly to find Casey searching the room for clues and taking down the rope. She slid the rope into an evidence bag, frowning. "Doubt I'll get any good prints from this."

"No," he agreed. "But there may be some on this ladder I found to remove the rope." He wondered aloud "Where could the rope have come from?"

She paused from snapping photos. "Ship's stores have plenty. Maybe we can lift some prints from the ladder, too."

"Stores are usually locked."

"But isn't the wine stored there for crew farewells and our Boxing Day dinner?"

"Right. I'd forgotten. Are we through here? The crew should be back from the mess soon."

"What will you do with his body?"

"I'll lug him to the walk-in freezer without meeting anyone on the way, I hope."

"Fine, Casey. Meet me in my cabin?"

Later in her cabin, they sat, staring at each other.

She was the first to say it. "Another murder! I can't believe t!"

He leaned back in his chair so far he almost fell backward. "Murder," he agreed.

Regaining his composure, he summarized. "In Park's case the murderer combined an uncanny knowledge of his target's fears with a trump card, that bottle of vodka. He hid that bottle under Park's pillow, knowing Park's alcohol problem.

"Hoosier's nightmares about Park, whom he saw jump overboard, were heightened by that rope noose he found hanging over his bunk. Somehow Hoosier was convinced that he could end his nightmares by following Park's imagined instructions. His 'way out' was to hang himself with that noose."

Kathlee opened the bottle of cognac with a flourish "Here," she handed him a tumbler. "We need this.

"By now we should be positive who the killer is," she stared at Casey. "We only have four possibilities left."

"Any usable prints on the rope or ladder…or anywhere?"

She bit her lip. "No, Casey. Also, no one claims to have removed the stores key from the bridge where it's kept. Avery and Tejada are there habitually on duty. Either could have taken a rope and knotted it into a noose.

"Avery was apoplectic when I told him about Hoosier. Says we can barely make it to Preparis Island, our next port with so small a crew. 'Our skeleton crew,' he keeps calling us."

Her telephone rang. "Skeleton crew, murder ship," she moaned. "What's next?"

Casey didn't voice the other vital question. Who is next?

She covered her ear as the phone continued to buzz. She answered his unspoken question with a look. "I'm not answering. I know it's my dad.

"You talk to him, Casey. Tell him I'm on the bridge or sleeping …or something."

Rolling his eyes, Casey answered the call. "Yes, Mr. Sigmund, this is Captain Flynn. Your daughter's fine but temporarily unavailable. She's very diligent about her duties, goes all over the ship, sir. Probably inspecting the engine room at this very moment.

"No, sir. We have yet to identify the murderer but I feel we're very close.

"Sir?" He turned to silently signal Kathlee in the corner. 'You owe me!'

He frowned at the next, although anticipated, question. "We have a crew total of five personnel, other than your daughter and myself, sir.

"Because of our personnel situation, she decided her first

duty is to remain aboard the *Bangor* to represent you and the company's interests.

"Yes, sir. I agree. She's very responsible and capable and, may I add, a delightful young lady."

At this, Kathlee covered her mouth to keep either from beaming or laughing. Then she leaned forward and kissed him on the cheek.

He motioned that she'd better stop. "I assure you, sir, I will safeguard your daughter at all costs.

"Eh? Yes, sir. And return her to you unharmed, of course."

Casey ruffled her hair, looking directly into azure eyes. "As soon as I see her, I'll ask her to return your call, Mr. Sigmund.

"My pleasure, sir. Yes, goodbye."

Kahlee released a long sigh. "Thanks, I very much appreciate that, especially the part about how delightful I am. Did he seem angry?"

"Father figures don't get angry. This father figure--that's me--intends to get even. So watch yourself, Miss Delightful."

Later she sat in the mess, sipping coffee with Alonzo. "I'm sorry to see you depressed, Papa."

He shrugged thick shoulders.

She continued. "This is the first time I've seen you not humming or singing a Marley tune.

"Are you unhappy, bunking with Partagas and the others in the sleeping bay? We thought you'd feel safer there."

Alonzo bobbed his head and stared into his coffee cup. "Yes, miss. I don't like being alone since…"

"I know," she assured him. "Hoosier's death frightens us all."

He cleared his throat. "You'll think me crazy, too, miss. But it's no fun…"

"What?"

Embarrassed, he closed his eyes. "Cooking for just a few

people. I'm used to preparing big meals for a dozen or more hungry men. Besides, nobody seems hungry around here anymore.

"I've worked for your father for almost eleven years, miss. Not sure I can stay here much longer. I got a family at home to provide for. I need a good, permanent job."

"This is a real, permanent job, Papa."

Alonzo cocked his head. "The way things are heading, there'll soon be nobody here to cook for. Then you sure won't need old Alonzo.

"I've have to move on. Can't forget my family. They depend on my pay."

"Stay with us, Papa," she implored. "Things will soon improve.

"I'm certain we can recruit some seamen at Preparis Island. Then you'll have plenty of hungry mouths to feed. Stick with us, Papa!"

Kathlee and Casey sat in her cabin, waiting to join the midnight shift in the mess hall. "Some shift!" she sighed. "Our entire crew is now down to six men."

She recounted the names on her fingers. "Avery and Tejada are on the bridge, Friauf and Suppe in the engine room."

She paused. "That leaves only Partagas and Alonzo, not including you and me. We've got to find and stop the killer before we're all dead!"

Casey took her hand in an increasingly familiar move. "After supper, I'm spending time below with Friauf and Suppe."

"Want to learn how to operate the turbines and pumps? I'll show you," she bragged.

"You," she fingered his shirt, "stay safe, hear?"

"You lock your door and keep that Glock pistol handy, **you** hear? I'll come by and check with you from time to time."

"Where do you intend to be?"

"Partagas has the deck patrol," he scratched his beard. "So I'll be everywhere as well as shadowing Partagas."

She patted him. "You safeguard **you** as well as Partagas."

A fusillade of hammering in the gangway made her jump from bed the next morning. She grabbed her robe and pistol.

"Dum, de, dum dum," she heard before cracking the door open.

Casey stood here balancing a tray of coffee cups and sweet rolls. "Alonzo baked these rolls especially for you this morning. You have charmed the cook, just as you have your captain."

She giggled. "Come in, charmed captain. Come in."

He set the tray on her small table and they took their usual chairs. "Sleep well?"

"No!" she answered. "Too many worries, you among them. That hammering convinced me I might as well get up. What's going on?"

"Partagas is installing the new sick bay door. Also," he held up a fistful of tools, "I'm installing an inside dead bolt on your cabin door."

"More safeguarding?" she grinned as she stirred her coffee. "How was your deck patrol or where ever?"

"Quiet and peaceful. If there was someone out there on deck, other than Partagas and me, I didn't sense it."

She buttered a roll. "Are we making good time toward our last drop at Preparis Island?"

"Karl Friauf says all well below. 'Steady and strong' he calls his diesels."

Suddenly the lights went out.

CHAPTER TWENTY ONE

BY THE TIME Casey reached the engine room, power was restored and several lights shining. Suppe sat at one of the consoles.

"One of the generator lines needs replacement, Captain," he answered Casey's look.

"Karl is over there, checking it out right now. He's our master electrician, you know."

"Hey!" The shout came from behind one of the huge 949 KVA generators.

"I'm back here without a light. Bring me a lantern. Quickly, please," Friauf yelled.

"Coming." Suppe responded, getting out of his chair and selecting a lantern from a locker.

"You should stay here, Captain," Suppe suggested. "It's very dark back there."

A scream negated Casey's answer. He and Suppe scrambled toward the sound.

Suddenly the silence nulled Casey's sense of direction.

"Where is he?"

Cursing, Suppe dropped the lantern, then stooped to retrieve it.

He pointed. "The scream seemed to come from the emergency generator back there."

Following Suppe in the darkness, Casey stumbled but kept his balance long enough to spot Friauf ahead.

The chief engineer lay on the metal grating in front of a small generator. For moments his body quivered from a gigantic electrical shock, then went limp.

Suppe bent down over Friauf. "My God! He's been electrocuted!

"Don't touch him! Back off!" Suppe instructed. "We need something nonconductive to pull him away."

Casey removed his big leather belt. "This ought to do it."

Hooking the belt around a leg, they dragged Friauf away from the generator.

Suppe stared at a loose connection wire sparking near Friauf's ankle. He pointed, "Look at that! A short!"

Casey took the lantern from Suppe and raised it above their heads. They stared at a small floor recess filled with water. "He must have slipped and his foot got into that water."

Suppe protested. "There is never any water in here! We keep it absolutely dry to avoid accidents."

Casey looked up at Suppe. "How did the water get there? I want you to trace that loose wire and see where it came from. Be careful!"

Minutes later, Casey knocked at Kathlee's door. "Bring your camera and evidence bags," he huffed from excitement.

"You won't believe it! We have another death, Karl Friauf!"

The four, Kathlee, Casey, Suppe and Avery, later sat at the mess table without speaking.

"Did he die instantly?" the First Mate wanted to know.

"Yes," she answered. "Instantly."

Rubbing his nose, Casey added, "Hopefully, it was painless."

"Tell us again what happened," Avery instructed Suppe.

Suppe hesitated, looking first at Casey and Kathlee.

"You are an engineer. You were there. Tell us again how this happened," Avery snapped.

Suppe leaned back on the bench. "As I said, one of the emergency generators had a momentary outage which Karl fixed. He must have wandered over to recheck it when the accident happened."

"Accident?" Casey questioned.

Kathlee looked up from her notes, "What exactly caused this 'accident'?

Suppe squirmed. "As best I can tell, there was a short in the coil connector assembly of the emergency generator which Karl discovered.

"While trying to fix it, he slipped into some water under the grating. To prevent falling, he must have accidentally grabbed a live wire. I'm repeating what I said earlier. There should be absolutely no water near the generators. None whatever."

Suppe stared at each of them around the table. "He accidentally grounded the short. That's all I can say, Captain."

The First Mate glowered. "We're no longer the 'murder ship' now we're the 'ghost ship' because of our lack of a crew."

Casey rubbed his forehead. "We'll put Partagas in the engine room to help Suppe. First Mate and I will work the bridge."

"That's possible," Avery admitted. "But who's going to discharge our cargo on arrival?"

"We'll all pitch in," Kathlee spoke up. "It'll take much longer but we can do it. Maybe we'll get lucky and hire some replacements."

The First Mate scowled. "Unless Preparis Island knows our 'murder'…no… 'ghost ship' reputation already."

"It's my fault," Casey spoke up. "I should have identified the murderer long before this. Now we have another loss, our chief engineer."

"Don't say that, Captain. Your security officer is to blame. I'm supposed to be security, not hospitality!

"I'm of the opinion that Friauf was murdered, Captain.

Seems strange, doesn't it?" she searched all their faces. "A master electrician makes a basic mistake he's been trained to avoid all his life? Even I know not to touch a live wire if I'm wet.

"Someone's trying to take over your vessel, Captain."

In her cabin, Kathlee wrote her report on Friauf's death after developing photos and re-reading Suppe's statement.

Casey knocked and entered at her response. He answered her questioning look. "I just carried Friauf to the walk-in cooler to keep Hoosier company until we reach Preparis."

"When will that be?" She eyed him holding aloft her father's old navigation compass.

"Another early morning arrival if the weather holds. ETA is approximately 0600." he said.

"You're admiring my brass compass?"

"Yes, and that's not all," he caressed a wayward lock of auburn hair.

"Concentrate, Casey," she shook her head. "Was Friauf's just a tragic accident or another damned murder?"

She peered at the keyboard in her lap. "What conclusion should I make in this report?"

"I'd call it 'death due to mysterious circumstances to be further investigated," Casey recited. "Suppe was quick to call it an accident but it could have been another carefully planned murder.

"Where did that water come from? Was it poured there to assure Friauf's death? Who did it?"

"Everyone on board has access to the engine room," she flexed her fingers.

"Except Alonzo. Which of the four remaining males is the most likely the mastermind and killer?"

"Dumb me, I still don't know!" He pressed hands to his forehead. "But Friauf's murder parodies the clever planning of the previous murders, doesn't it?"

"Maybe, but I still need a motive," she said. "Let's review our plans for arrival tomorrow morning. We don't have enough manpower to work our cargo once we dock. I'll go ashore and try to recruit some longshoremen to help us unload the deck cargo, then reload the new deck cargo for Singapore."

Casey nodded at her expertise. "You sound like a skipper already, Kathlee. Since we empty our last oil tank in Preparis, we need plenty of deck cargo to keep the ship from wallowing."

She was absorbed with the new manifest. "We're picking up twelve thousand cases of Nicaraguan rum called *Flor de Managua*. Did you know that?"

"Whew! That's a lot of rum! Wait. What are you doing?"

Hefting a pair of scissors, she stepped behind his chair. "I'm trimming your hair and beard before supper, Casey. Don't squirm if you want to keep both ears!"

"Look here, Second Mate." First Mate Avery always used Tejada's title whenever he had a chore for him.

"You and I have to do something about this crisis. We can't continue like this. If you're depending on our dizzy new captain or that female security officer to handle this, **forget it!**

"Those two couldn't find their asses with both hands! Besides they seem to be lovey-dovey. No wonder they aren't paying attention to what's going on here.

"We've got to stop the murder of our crew!"

"What can we do, First Mate?"

"How's this sound?" Avery almost whispered. "To save this ship and what remains of our crew, we pull into the nearest port...and ask for help."

"Help from who? Tejada smirked. "Who's going to take our word about this rotten situation over that of the captain and security officer?"

"We go to the police chief and ask him to place armed officers aboard the good ole *Bangor* to keep the peace."

"And?"

"Then you and I are at least safe, right?"

Gaining confidence in his idea, Avery rubbed his hands together. "Then we persuade the police to send a cable back to the *Seatrans* head office to ask for help. Then you and I are off the blame line and it's up to Bridgetown to solve this nightmare!

"What do you think, Second Mate?"

Tejada shrugged. "Don't think it would work as easily as you claim. I say we just jump ship at the next port. Then appeal to *Seatrans* to find us new jobs. Get us off this damned murder ship permanently!"

CHAPTER TWENTY TWO

S HE POUNDED ON Casey's cabin door at 0500 the next morning. Although bedraggled from his patrolling until 0300, he still opened the door with a grin. He stood aside, holding the familiar blanket in place.

"What's that hammering?" she asked, extending two coffee cups and resisting a giggle as he struggled with the blanket.

He offered her a chair while juggling coffee with one hand, blanket in the other. "Last night Partagas told me he had yet to finish installing that new sick room door. Guess he's doing that now."

"You must be getting to know him pretty well from patrolling the main deck. Any shadowy figures watching you last night?"

Casey gulped down half his coffee and reached for clothing. "Let's join our tiny crew for breakfast, if you're ready."

He paused. "Aren't you going to at least turn your back while I finish dressing?"

Arms akimbo, she stood her ground. "I see no reason to do so. Aren't you capable of doing two things at once? Meanwhile, I want to tell you my proposition."

Casey stopped. "My answer is 'yes'! If I am guessing your proposition, I'm shedding these trousers right now!"

She laughed. "Whoa! Wrong proposition!

"I propose we go to the hiring hall after breakfast and hire at least four longshoremen to work as deck crew for the day. Our regular guys get a half-day off."

Wincing, he buttoned his shirt. "What happens to our two corpses in the walk-in cooler?"

"I've ordered a mortuary van to meet us on the pier at eleven. Once that's done, we go to the police with my reports about their deaths."

Casey grinned. "By the time we return after all that, I'm hoping to hear a much different proposition from you, Miss Sigmund."

"If that's your idea of 'sweet talk,' Captain," she stared at him, "don't expect a positive response from me!"

Grinning with satisfaction, Kathlee trailed the four workmen she just hired across the pier and up the *Bangor's* temporary gangway. Guessing the new men would more naturally follow Casey than herself, she was the last person aboard.

She flourished the employment office's list of names in Casey' face once they were seated in her cabin. "Recruiting them was easy," she gloated. "Must have been my professional, business-like attitude."

"Plus, you looked splendid herding them down the pier in those killer jeans

"Or was it the Singapore dollars you offered them, professional charmer? Whatever it was," Casey grinned, clapping his hands, "I applaud your efforts!

"Your success again raises the question. Why was Second Mate Tejada so often a failure at recruiting? I wonder if he really made the effort ?"

Kathlee added "If not, why not, eh? Let's go on deck and see how he's managing those new workers."

Tejada stood impatiently by the cargo derrick, anxious to begin the work of unloading the deck cargo of pharmaceuticals and, finally, filling the empty deck with twelve thousand cases of Nicaraguan rum.

Kathlee imagined Tejada's toothy grin contained a glint of envy. She had managed to find workers. The Second Mate had not.

She handed Tejada the list of names and the pay receipts each new man would sign once work was completed. Immediately he gave curt orders to the men, first assigning them tasks to hook the big oil discharge hoses to couplings on the pier. That begun, he told Alonzo and Partagas to return to their regular duties.

Casey pointed. "The mortuary van has arrived. I'll use Partagas to bring the bodies out the delivery door without the new hires or our crew seeing them."

She patted his newly-trimmed beard. "You, Captain, are looking just like an admiral today."

He grinned in embarrassment, turning aside to conceal it. "I'll meet you on the pier once I have mortuary receipts for the bodies."

Later they spent two hours at the police station reviewing her reports on the deaths of Houser and Friauf. On the way back to their ship, Casey insisted on treating her to an impromptu lunch at a sidewalk café.

"I ate too much," she complained as she later climbed the temporary gangway. Casey paused, studying the new hires at work. "Wonder where Partagas is? I thought he'd be out here working the new guys."

They climbed the stairs to their cabins. "Probably Partagas is helping Suppe in the engine…."

Her voice changed to a shriek. "Look!" she pointed at a prone body in the passageway.

"It's Partagas!"

The body lay beside the sick room's new door, clutching a

screwdriver in one hand. An array of loose screws on the floor circled his other palm.

A puddle of blood formed another circle about his head. Red oozed from a deep gash in the back of the young sailor's head.

"Oh, no! Not Partagas!" Casey kneeled beside the still form to check for breathing and pulse.

Slowly he stood, shaking his head. "He's gone."

Kathlee collapsed. "God, Casey," she cried. "Why can't we stop this slaughter?"

He lifted her to her feet, opened her cabin door and gently guided her to a bunk. "Close your eyes," he whispered. "I must leave you for a minute but I'll be back soon. I'm locking your door so don't worry."

Stoically, he returned to Partagas' body and began snapping photos with her camera. Just feet away, he noticed a bloody hammer discarded after the fatal blow. He picked it up with an evidence bag turned inside out.

Coming down the stairs from the galley, Alonzo skidded to a stop at the sight of Casey, "Lunch is over, Captain, but I can make you a sand…

"Holy God! Is he dead?"

In a choked voice, Casey whispered. "Your captain has failed to prevent another murder, Papa!"

On the bridge, Tejada added the huge rum inventory to the ship's manifest. Not wanting to discuss Partagas' murder, Casey returned to Kathlee's cabin.

"Dum, de, dum, dum," he announced as he knocked on her door and stepped inside. Stuck beneath the door was an envelope addressed to her.

As he entered, Kathlee sat up on the side of her bunk and gave him a brave smile.

He handed her the envelope.

"What's this?" she blinked at her name scrawled on it.

"Can't be good news," he stared at it and sat down beside her.

Moodily, she stretched. "I've got to get busy and write up that report on Partagas' murder." She set the strange envelope aside on the table.

Staring at it, curiosity won and she opened and quickly read its few sentences. After a moment, she handed it to Casey.

He began reading it aloud. "Dear Miss…"

He skipped to the signature at the bottom. "It's from Alonzo!"

Nodding, she closed her eyes. "Go ahead. Read it all."

Thinking he had never seen Kathlee so distraught, he read it aloud.

"I am a coward to leave you like this, but I must survive for the sake of my family.

Partagas' murder made up my mind. I'm sorry to desert you. I now feel certain that I'll be the next to be killed if I stay here.

"So long. Please don't remember me as a deserter and coward.

"God bless you and your father. I worked for him for eleven years.

"Signed, Alonzo.

"P.S. I left a pot of stew and a dozen sandwiches in the galley."

At the bottom of the page, a Singapore address was scribbled with the notation,

"In case you want to mail me any last wages."

CHAPTER TWENTY THREE

AS IF THIS were their last supper, the five-man crew of the *Bangor*, sat silently eating warmed soup and cheese sandwiches.

To encourage conversation, Kathlee asked "When do we sail for our next port-of-call, Captain?"

Casey smiled at her effort. "Just as soon as we can hire another cook--unless everyone's happy with this grub?"

This evoked an immediate shaking of heads and groans.

At the end of the table, Tejada raised his head from his soup.

"If we don't all pitch-in with extra duties, we'll never make Singapore. Ain't that right, Captain?"

"That's right," Casey looked at each person. "We've got to keep the old *Bangor* afloat and engines running. We still have deck cargo to deliver and customers to satisfy."

"If we are to have jobs this time tomorrow," Kathlee added.

Casey tapped on her door after the supper. They sat in their usual places on opposite sides of her small table.

"You look weary, Casey," she began.

"You, too," he touched her hair. "Are you not sleeping well?"

With that she placed the cognac bottle and glasses on the table. Concentrating, she poured careful drinks. "That meal in the mess really seemed like a last supper, didn't it?"

He answered with a question. "Any good fingerprints on that bloody screwdriver?"

"No," she raised her glass. "The murder weapon was probably something else, like a hammer."

"Easily disposed of by throwing it overboard?"

"Right. The killer may habitually wear gloves. Maybe we need to search the ship for an incriminating pair and see who they fit."

"Great, but we have no one spare to search. All of us are necessary to get us out of this port."

She stared at his black clothing. "Why are you dressed in black? Trying to depress me or your faithful crew?"

He sipped the cognac appreciatively. "I should have worn this outfit sooner. Remember I intended earlier to offer myself as bait?"

She sighed. "At least our suspect list is quite short. With Alonzo gone, we have only Suppe, Tejada, you and I. Short list! Which of us is the killer?"

"That's why I want you to be super cautious," he implored. "After I step out your door this evening, please keep the door double locked and your pistol handy.

"Don't allow anyone in, **despite the pretense. Only me.**"

"And you?" she countered. "What do you hope to accomplish in that commando outfit? Where's your pistol?"

He stood, drained his glass with a thank-you, and tapped his side "You have water here, your I-phone, and I brought you a sack of canned goods from the galley.

"Stay safe, Kathlee. I'll be back as soon as I can."

He half-waved as he snapped her door shut behind him.

A voice whispered. "Do you see that?"

"He's walking the deck by himself. Here's our chance!"

"Let's get him!"

He crept along the starboard rail toward the forecastle, pausing to check behind him while listening for footsteps or voices.

Casey reasoned that he was the last obstacle preventing the murderer or murderers gaining complete control of his ship. He gambled that he was the next, probably last, target.

If he were killed, he fought back thoughts of what might happen to Kathlee.

Forget that, he told himself. Find out tonight who is the killer determined to control the *Bangor* by eliminating its crew…and why.

He reached the forecastle bulkhead without hearing or seeing any sign of another person. Quietly, he slid down the port side, only stopping to position the pistol better in his waistband.

The sky was dark and cloudy, the prevailing wind coming from the starboard quarter. For several minutes he kneeled in the shadow of the forward ventilator and waited.

Waiting is my forte, he thought to himself. I've waited for years to command a vessel and now I've done it…but not for long if I'm careless tonight.

Not hearing or seeing anything, he backtracked along the port side, and slipped down the starboard rail toward the massive stacks of rum cases secured on the deck.

In the shadow of the rum cases, he waited. And waited.

Still he detected no noise or suspicious shapes. Avoiding the dim light from the bridge windows, he crossed an open sliver of deck to the mooring gears beneath the ship's funnel.

He about-faced and tiptoed forward toward the lifeboat hoist.

That was a mistake

Someone hiding beneath the ladder hit him on the back of the head, spinning him around with such force that he was breathless and near unconscious.

Another shadow appeared beside him and clubbed the pistol from his hand.

Despite the terrific pain from his head, he heard one shadow order the other. "Help me drag him over to the rail on this tarp. Then we'll heave him overboard."

Momentarily, Casey imagined he was on his cabin bunk with a bad headache.

"Heavier than he looks. Help me. Grab a leg."

Clasping the tarp as if it were his familiar bunk mattress, he felt himself being lifted, and heaved over the side of the vessel. He both felt and heard the sting of cold sea water enfolding him.

Had he been clear headed, he might have heard the voices on the deck far above him.

"Hooray! Sweet dreams, Captain! We're glad to finally be rid of you, Let's go tell the princess and see her reaction."

Heavy knocking on her door frightened Kathlee. The caller clearly was not Casey returning from his rounds. She began pushing furniture against the door as a barricade.

"Open up, Princess!" a voice whooped.

Another cackled, "We have important news for you, darling!"

She pulled a chair opposite the pile of furniture she'd stacked against the door, sat and levered a cartridge into the pistol chamber.

Silence is best, she decided once she was seated, trying to control her breathing, pistol in hand, hammer cocked.

If they break down the door, she'd shoot to kill, she calmly decided.

If not, she'd sit here, ready but hoping they would eventually tire of their antics and go away.

Despite her deliberate preparations, Kathlee felt herself shuddering. The next voice added to her fright.

"We want to tell you that your boyfriend is missing, Princess."

Another voice snickered. "He went for a little midnight swim."

"We'll see you at breakfast, Princess. Then it'll be time for you decide which of us will be your new boyfriend!"

"More likely, both of us!" The men outside whooped as they left.

She alternately sobbed and attempted to contact her father on her I-phone. The steel structure of the bridge directly over her cabin prevented contact.

For the remainder of a sleepless night, she kept trying to establish telephonic contact with anyone, anywhere, without success.

A dominant, depressing thought kept repeating.

"Casey is dead. Casey is dead."

On the bridge, Avery and Tejada quarreled while drinking left-over coffee. Avery berated Tejada for allowing Alonzo leave the ship in Preparis.

"Terrible coffee!" Avery contined to complain. Moving to the gyro compass, he studied its face.

He exploded. "I told you to maintain a course of sixty degrees until we clear the Cayos! This heading is forty-five, not sixty!"

Tejada decided to pour himself more coffee. "I bet the signal mast sensor is cluttered again and giving false readings.

"Maybe we should go up there and check it, Captain," he used Avery's new title, but made no move to leave the bridge.

Livid, Avery shook his fist. "You got that right, Conejo! I am now the captain and master of this vessel. **You** get outa' here, climb up there and check it.

"Aye, aye, sir." Tejada stood but stopped.

"But Captain, sir," Tejada sat down again. "I broke my glasses on Great Coco. I won't be able to see well enough to give you an accurate report, sir."

Avery paced to the compass and back. "Then we'll both climb up there and take a look. C'mon!"

Gesturing that Avery should precede him, Tejada paused. A second later he followed Avery up the narrow fifty foot ladder leading to the top of the mast.

"Watch your step, sir," Tejada cautioned as they reached the pinnacle.

As Avery reached for the top rung of the ladder, Tejada grabbed the back of Avery's belt and jerked backwards as hard as he could.

Looking over his shoulder, Tejada grinned as Avery fell, screaming. The scream ended abruptly with Avery sprawled on top of the bridge castle.

Tejada leaned out, spat toward the crumpled form, and smiled beatifically.

"**Captain** Tejada! I love the sound of that!"

CHAPTER TWENTY FOUR

BACK ON THE bridge, Tejada marched back and forth in his new domain. Stopping beside the engine order recorder, he sent his first order.

Needlessly, he also called the engineer officer on the telephone. "Did you get my signal?"

"Yeah," came back a gruff, just awakened voice. "Ahead one-third. What's up?"

Donning the captain's binoculars, Tejada scanned a small island off the port bow. "We're almost at our rendezvous point. Might as well save fuel. Slow to stand-by."

"Are we dropping anchor?"

"No, we may need to maneuver a bit. Just enough power to keep us steady. Got it?"

"Aye, ave, Captain."

Elated by the engineer's use of his new title, Tejada felt generous. "Might as well come up to the mess. We'll have coffee and whatever we can find to eat."

"Is the princess still hiding in her cabin?"

"Yeah, but she'll come out and be friendly once she's hungry"

"I'm going to enjoy sharing a bottle of wine with her."

"Then bring the wine up with you. I'm thirsty, too."

Once seated in the now deserted mess, the two men poured themselves coffee laced with vodka and ate cheese sandwiches.

"Wonder if she can cook?"

"We'll find if she can cook as well as she looks in dungarees."

"Or without them," Suppe chortled.

"Business first," Tejada rubbed his nose. "How are the engines?"

"Steady and regular as always," Suppe boasted.

Tejada nodded. "Fine. The tender should be here within an hour or so. Its crew will transfer our deck cargo to it. That may take some time, depending on the size of their crew."

Suppe rubbed his eyes. "Tell me again how much our cut will be, Captain."

"Well, we are promised US$300. per case. That times twelve thousand cases means we get…"

Tejada grinned at the other "Well … you do the math."

Suppe whooped. "Three point six million dollars split between us. Equally, right?"

Tejada nodded an answer.

Suppe was ecstatic. "That P2P stuff must make a lot of meth!"

Tejada's grin vanished. "Yeah. The mysterious boss of this heist will profit immensely. I can't even imagine the street value of the meth which can be made from the P2P in those fake cases of Nicaraguan rum."

Suddenly, Tejada rose and smashed his fist against the mess table, spilling both coffees. "He'll make many millions while we only get a *pequena* taste of that sweet money! And we did all the dangerous part!

"Wish I knew who he is. Anyway, I'm going to ask for more…much more for our hard work!"

Suppe gloated. "We're going to be rich…very rich men. I'll retire to Panama!"

Frowning, Tejada cautioned. "We've got to be very careful."

"Why? You don't trust our big boss, whoever he is?"

"Wake up, Suppe. The whole crew on that tender will be

armed. What if the boss decides to knock us off after the cargo is on his deck? He'll keep the whole $3.6 million!

"All we have to defend ourselves is that pistol I took from Flynn while we were tossing him overboard. By the way, where is it?"

Suppe extracted a pistol from his trousers and held it up. "Right here!"

Tejada's expression changed as he studied the pointed pistol.

"Okay. Here's what we do. We count the money before a single case is transferred to the tender. No money, no transfer."

Dubious about the odds of an armed crew versus his one pistol, Suppe wrinkled his forehead. "I'll use the pistol if I have to. I won't just show it. I'll use it."

Tejada held out his hand. "Better let me decide when to use it, partner. I'm the captain."

Suppe held the pistol loosely in his lap. "Not so fast, Captain Conejo. If I give you the pistol, what keeps you from shooting me and keeping the entire $3.6 million?"

Tejada extended his hand farther. "We're shipmates, buddy! You know you can trust old Conejo here. We've gotten this far together, haven't we? Hasn't everything worked out just as we planned?

"Tell you what," Tejada reflected. "Give me the pistol and you get the girl first."

Suppe stood, brandishing the pistol. "Think I'm stupid? Then you'll shoot me, get the girl and all the money!"

Tejada's sharp blade caught Suppe under the left jaw and severed his throat to below the right ear.

Blinking his eyes in surprise at his gushing blood, Suppe managed to point the pistol as he slid to the floor.

He fired once.

Tejada yelled in pain and surprise. Tumbling forward, he lay motionless on the floor except for shivering.

Blood spurting from his throat, Suppe tried to keep from sliding downward. Finally he failed and fell facedown alongside Tejada.

The only sound was the stand-by drone of the turbine engines below.

CHAPTER TWENTY FIVE

CASEY ROLLED OUT from under the galley's skirted food preparation table where he heard Tejada talk about the planned rendezvous with the traffickers.

Stiff muscles from hiding under the table ached, but he hurried to the mess, staring briefly at the two bodies.

"Thank you, gentlemen," he said after checking them for life. "You've solved the problem of how I capture the two of you," he muttered, scooping up his pistol and the binoculars.

He rushed down the companionway to Kathlee's cabin, calling her name. "Kathlee, Kathlee! It's Casey!"

Disbelieving, she shrieked, "Casey! Is it really you? I thought I'd lost you!"

"Hurry!" he called before the door could be cleared on her side. "We've got to get to the bridge right away!"

In minutes--which seemed much longer--she shoved aside the barricade enough to open her jammed door.

"Casey, Casey!" Her embrace almost knocked him off his bare feet.

She both laughed and cried. "They told me you were gone...that I'd never see you again."

He held her so tightly that neither could breathe. Then, at arm's length, he asked "Are you hurt? What did those two do to you?"

"I'm fine. What happened to you? Where are they? They boasted they threw you overboard."

"Get your Glock, any extra ammunition you have and your I-phone. We've got to get on the bridge and prepare ourselves for an invasion."

She paused from kissing him again. "Prepare for what?"

He spoke faster. "We're in danger! The *Bangor* is about to be boarded by armed gangsters who are after our deck cargo."

Reaching the bridge, he surveyed the nearby waters with the binoculars for an oncoming tender.

"Quick! Use your I-phone and make a distress call--an SOS."

"What's happening, Casey?" She held her phone outside the bridge attempting to contact the Indian navy, police or anyone.

"That deck cargo isn't rum. It's some kind of precursor to make methamphetamine. Controlling it and the ship was the reason for all those murders."

She hesitated. "Are you sure? I saw the *Flor de Managua* shipping invoices and they looked genuine."

"I'm certain," he replied, putting the binoculars down so he could hug her as she punched her phone.

"The fake rum cases were filled with something called P2P. Selling it to drug traffickers for a huge profit motivated Tejada and Suppe to attempt to take over our ship by killing everybody.

"With all of us dead, they could sell the P2P without interference.

"Oh, no," he leaned forward. "I see a small craft approaching. Could be the traffickers coming for the P2P. It's coming too fast for anything else."

"Kathlee, can you really handle the diesels down below? We're going to need full power in a minute or two."

She grinned. "Sure, I can handle the diesels, just like I said. But we can't outrun them, can we?"

"If those gangsters get aboard, they'll kill us and take the P2P. They might even sink our ship.

"Our options are to try to fight them off--and they probably have lots of weapons--or we could run the ship aground. Still they'd get aboard and kill us for the P2P.

"I have another idea, maybe not the best, but it might save us."

"What?" She held the I-phone askew. "The police are on the line and want to know where we are."

"Hooray! Tell them we're about two miles off the east coast of Preparis Island. We can see the lighthouse on the eastern tip of that island.

"Tell them to hurry!

"Quick! Get those diesels humming. If the traffickers give us a good target, I'll ask you for full power, full speed. We'll cut 'em in two!"

She hugged him with one arm, still talking to the police, before dashing below.

Alone, he studied the approaching tender. A half-dozen armed men stood on the tender's deck, waving.

"They're expecting a friendly welcome from Tejada," he growled, then leaned forward to return their waves.

He removed the magazine from his pistol and counted the remaining cartridges. Seven.

"C'mon!" He waved again. "A friendly welcome from the *Bangor* awaits you! C'mon!"

Suddenly the friendly waves from the tender turned into rifle fire ricocheting against the bridge beside Casey's head. Looking through the binoculars again, he saw the reason.

Alonzo, his former cook, stood on the tender deck wearing a new Panama hat. He recognized Casey and ordered his men to shoot him.

"Alonzo!" Casey mumbled. "He's in this, too!

118

"Seeing me on the bridge, he realizes his heist is in jeopardy!"

He used the intercom to alert Kathlee in the engine room below. "Are you ready?"

"Aye, aye, Captain," she hooted. "We're ready for full power at your command."

"Wait, wait," he spoke into the intercom while peering over the rail.

"Closer, closer..." he urged the tender.

The tender cut its engines and began heaving to, its hull rhythmically bouncing from the momentum of the wake.

"Now!" Casey yelled into the intercom. "Full power!"

If an aged oil tanker can leap from the water, the *Bangor* did, as its diesels screamed at maximum power.

The startled faces at the tender's rail immediately reacted to their danger by jumping off the beams. Their weapons filled the air like startled gulls, then splashed into the water.

Mesmerized, the captain of the tender tried to twist his wheel sharply away from the tanker's dark hull only a few feet away. He gunned his single engine, but too late.

The last Casey saw of Alonzo--former cook, now boss trafficker--was his new Panama hat floating jauntily in the bow wake.

The *Bangor* impacted the thin-hulled tender with a sickening crash and kept plowing through the debris to open water.

Casey's last memory was a repeat of his earlier being throw overboard by Tejada and Suppe. This time the force of the impact between tanker and tender ejected him from his perch on the bridge. He landed on a hatch cover below, unconscious.

CHAPTER TWENTY SIX

S HE KNOCKED AND entered the hospital room with a flourish. Instead of her usual seaman's garb, she wore a frilly blue skirt, white blouse and gold sandals.

"Feeling any better, Casey?"

He sat upright in bed, supported by several oversized pillows. Upon seeing her, he whistled, holding out his arms.

"Wonder woman! You're a beautiful sight!"

Kathlee pulled a chair closer and leaned forward to kiss his forehead.

"You're a brick, Casey, to have--one-- survived being thrown overboard into the dark sea by Suppe and Tejada, and—two--being ejected from the bridge unto a steel deck.

"Feel up to telling me how you endured all that and can still smile?"

He couldn't stop grinning. "Are we in the naval hospital in George Town?"

"Did I ever tell you," he reminisced, "that George Town is named for an old English relative of mine, circa, 1600?"

"No, Casey, Is that where you got those rascally genes?"

His grin vanished. "More importantly, are **you** alright? Any injuries from those killers or from handling those powerful engines of the good ole *Bangor*?"

"I'm fine, thank you," she became serious. "In fact, I'm ready to signal your engines 'Ahead full,' as you did me when the traffickers approached."

He chuckled at the innuendo. "My engines won't idle much longer, sweetie."

Casey changed tone. "What happened to our *Bangor?*"

"Also fine," she reported. "Just a scar on the bow. Daddy's sending us a relief crew to run the *Bangor,*" she reported with a special smile.

"You," she wiggled a finger at him, "are ordered to fly back to Bridgetown to report our status directly to my father."

"Sounds to me like you're being groomed to be the next captain of the *Bangor* since I messed it up." He studied her face.

"Congratulations, Kathlee! What happened to those traffickers and Alonzo on the tender we sunk?"

"The Navy picked up five survivors. The others were lost in the collision."

Patting her hand on the white hospital sheets, he widened his eyes. "Sorry about Alonzo. I know you liked Alonzo although he turned out to be enemy number one."

"What about him, Casey?"

"I have unhappy news for you. Papa Alonzo was on that tender with about six armed men who he ordered to shoot me off the bridge. He realized if I were on the bridge, something was wrong with his big drug deal.

"So he told his thugs to shoot me just before we cut that tender in two when you goosed our engines to full forward. We cut his little boat in half and he and lots of his men were lost in the collision.

"Good old Alonzo, our friendly, caring cook, was the mastermind of the plan to seize our ship and its cargo by killing all our crew. Sorry."

He thought for a moment before speaking. "Suppe and Tejadad didn't even know Alonzo was the boss of the operation to take over our ship!"

She shook her tousled hair. "No, Casey! I can't believe that about Papa Alonzo. Not Papa!"

He handed her a tissue from the bed stand. After a moment he tried to change the mood.

"What happened to all that P2P the traffickers were after?"

She wiped her nose and leaned on his chest. "Some investigator from George Town will receive a handsome reward from the government for that huge seizure.

"Speaking of trafficking, I must complete the rest of those reports for the police. Let's start with how you survived being thrown overboard by Suppe and Tejada that night."

"Do I have to?" he pled.

"Yes, you must, Casey."

He began recounting his nightmare. "Suppe hit me on the back of the head so hard, I dreamed I was falling out of my bunk. Strange, eh?

"Unconsciously, I must have grabbed at the imaginary bunk as I hit the water. Luckily, I caught a loose line hanging from our lowered accommodation ladder.

"I spent an hour hanging on that ladder until I was sure Tejada and Suppe were satisfied I was a goner. Then I climbed back aboard and hid in the galley."

"Why there?"

"I was happy to be anywhere! The food preparation table in the galley has a little curtain around it so I crawled under the table. More luck, eh?"

She touched his lower lip with a finger. "I was frantic after they yelled they had thrown you overboard!"

He kissed the finger. "Sorry, but I couldn't be seen by them after I made it out of the water."

Kathlee took her eyes off him to jot a few notes on her pad. "Different subject. When did you decide to ram the traffickers' tender?"

Casey shrugged. "I couldn't think of another way to save our lives. If those traffickers boarded us, I knew we would be shot or just thrown overboard."

She applied a cold towel to his forehead. "Does it still ache from falling on the deck from the bridge when we rammed the tender?"

He leaned forward. "A kiss on the lips would make me remarkably better."

Four hours later they sat at her table, finishing the bottle of wine found in the galley.

He caressed her hand. "Why does your father wants me to personally report to him in Bridgetown?"

"I asked him that over the telephone, dear. He wouldn't say. He's been angry with me ever since I didn't scurry to him in Bridgetown earlier.

"He's a dear, but once he's made up his mind, he's hard to change. I know from experience.

"Maybe, just maybe, he plans to give you a bigger vessel. Wouldn't that be great? You'll need a security officer and I know one who's available immediately."

Casey held up a hand. "Why not come with me to Bridgetown to see him? Two birds with one…"

She interrupted. "I asked that as well, dear. He wants a company representative aboard the *Bangor* at all times to deny any salvage claim from the local government.

"Don't worry. Wherever you are, I'll be there. Even if I have to follow you to Timbuktu!"

On the way to the airport, she pressed a small wooden case into his hand.

"What's this?" he studied the little box.

"Oh," he recognized it. "Your father's old brass compass. The one he gave you for your first solo voyage, to keep you safe and on course. And it worked!"

She blinked back tears. "Yes, darling. I want you to have

it. Keep it with you always. I pray it will bring you back to me, 'safe and on course."

As the taxi stopped in front of the terminal, he kissed her again and again.

"Let's not have a tearful airport goodbye inside. I'll telephone you as soon as I see your father in Bridgetown with some, I hope, good news!

"Farewell for the moment, darling. Until 'dum, de, dum, dum!"

With that, he disappeared into the airport.

CHAPTER TWENTY SEVEN

"CAPTAIN CASEY FLYNN of the *Bangor* reporting, sir!" His first surprise was the lack of a smile or an invitation to sit. Mr. Sigmund, CEO and owner of *Seatrans*, stiffly stood behind a massive desk, staring at him. A warm, welcoming greeting was also absent.

Instead, the first words Casey heard were "As of this moment, you are no longer a captain in my company, **Mister Flynn. Nor are you employed by Seatrans!**

"That out of the way, listen carefully to what I'm about to say. It will be short and simple, I promise.

"I'm firing you because of your several extremely serious, even criminal, mistakes which I cannot--will not--forgive. The first is the safety of my daughter.

"You were culpably negligent in not safeguarding her during your captaincy. She was endangered several times. One such terrible time you were even off the vessel. You deserted her, alone, to the mercies of two armed and dangerous thugs. Thank heavens she was quick enough to lock them out temporarily. Otherwise, they might have gang-raped, even killed her! I place full blame you for that terrible situation and the trauma she will always retain, Mister Flynn!

"Secondly, during the short term of your captaincy, the members of your crew were being mysteriously murdered. It was your duty as captain to keep your crew safe, just as it was to safeguard my daughter. You failed miserably at both.

"You chose to ram and sink a smaller vessel which, up to that point, had only approached the *Bangor* in international waters. Serious loss of life to the crew of the smaller ship resulted from your poor judgment and rash action.

"My company may be sued for the cost of that vessel which I am told was a tender. An even larger lawsuit may develop for the loss of life of that crew as a result of your hasty action."

Speechless at this bitter barrage, Casey stared dumbly at Sigmund, father of the woman to whom he intended to propose marriage as soon as he could.

"My attorneys advise me that we may also be criminally responsible for your negligence. Your cargo contained a massive amount of dangerous, illegal drugs of great value. Thank goodness those drugs eventually were seized by the Indian navy.

"The only living eye witnesses who can positively identify that cargo of drugs are yourself and my daughter. I will not, of course, ask her to give evidence in a court of law to your perfidy.

"There remains what should I do with you, Mr. Flynn, former employee?

"In a few minutes, you will be escorted by armed guard to the airport and placed upon a flight to Port Blair in the Andamans. At the airport gate you will be given your boarding pass as you enter the aircraft, not before.

"Once at Port Blair, you will find a small skipjack awaiting you at dockside already registered in your name and provisioned. That represents your final pay from my company. I hope you will board that vessel and sail away to Xanadu, Never-Never Land or where ever the westward winds carry you. **Never to return!**

"Finally, I ask for your word that you will never see or contact my daughter again. I do not intend to tell her of your departure or destination. I hope she interprets your absence as a total lack of interest on your part.

"Do I have your word?"

Outraged yet numb, Casey ignored the question. He stomped out of the room to be immediately hustled into a waiting sedan.

An hour later, Kathee called her father. "Is Casey there yet?"

"No, dear," he lied. "Haven't seen him."

She repeated her call every day during waking hours for an entire week with the same answer.

EPILOGUE

A MONTH LATER, SHE called her father's chauffer to wish him happy retirement.

"Hello, Jerome. This is Kathlee, hoping your retirement party today is all you wish it to be. I know how faithfully you worked for my father all these years. Saying 'thank you' is not nearly sufficient but it will have to do until I see you again in Bridgetown."

"Thank you, Miss Kathlee. Your words are particularly satisfying since I've had the privilege of seeing you grow into a fine young lady over the years I served your father. You certainly make him proud!

"I've lost track of you lately. Where are you now? Still on that old, rusty *Bangor?*"

"Right you are. Dad wants me to gain command experience, so I'll be on the Singapore to Rangoon circuit for six months.

"May I ask you a peculiar question, Jerome?"

"You know you can, Miss Kathlee. Anything."

"Well," she hesitated, "do you know anything about Captain Casey Flynn, a very good friend of mine? Like, where is he? What's he doing? My father won't tell me anything about Captain Flynn for some reason."

Jerome caught his breath, hesitating, considering how to honestly answer.

Finally, he replied after assuring himself no one was within hearing.

"Since I retired from your father's service today, I feel I can tell you now, whereas a day ago, I might not."

Her anguish was painful and evident. "Oh, Jerome! Have you seen him? Where is he? Is he alright?" The questions kept tumbling out.

He took an even deeper breath. "Miss Kathlee, if you reveal to anyone what I'm about to say...well, my hard-earned retirement pay will vanish! Do you understand? Jerome's old goose would be cooked to a deep hue."

"I understand completely, Jerome. I would die rather than betray you. Yes, I know my father can be very vindictive."

Now it was her time for a deep breath. "Where is he, Jerome?"

"Is Port Blair still one of your customers?"

She caught her breath. "Yes. Is he there? So close and he didn't contact me?"

"Let me tell you what little I know, Miss. A month or so ago I received very detailed instructions to drive a gentleman to the airport and personally watch him get on an airplane bound for Port Blair.

"I was accompanied by two strangers whose job was to assure the gentlemen boarded the plane, in case he tried to change his mind. I also noticed that both these strangers were armed. One held the gentleman's boarding pass until he actually entered the airplane's door. The other stranger just walked alongside the gentleman, one hand on his shoulder, saying nothing.

"Very strange, what?"

"Strange indeed, Jerome. Was that gentleman Captain Flynn?"

"Yes, ma'm, it was."

"Did he appear to be ill? Did he act normally despite his peculiar escort of two armed men?"

"He looked normal to me. But I was told **not** to speak to him. Very strange, as I said."

She waited a second. "Can you tell me anything else?"

"Well...let's see. One man had the Captain's boarding pass in his hand. The other man carried a folio of papers which he handed the Captain as he boarded the airplane."

Jerome scratched his head, looked up seeing his homeward bus approaching.

"There was one other thing. Nobody referred to the gentleman as 'Captain.' Apparently, he was no longer a captain, Miss.

"My jitney bus is here and I must catch it to get home today. Hope what I said is helpful. Old Jerome says 'Goodbye, Miss!'"

She immediately went ashore to the telephone exchange to place a call to the Harbor Master of Port Blair.

"Hello. This is Captain Sigmund of the *Bangor* calling. I'm trying to locate a small vessel missing from the *Seatrans* fleet. I do not know the name of the vessel. It could easily have been changed. The registered owner is an individual named Casey Flynn.

"Can you help me, please?"

"Can you hold on, Captain? Looking up by the owner's name may take a few minutes."

"Thank you very much. Yes, I can hold."

Minutes later, the Harbor Master whooped. "Success!

"I found such a vessel and registry. It was so recent an addition to our data base that I should have remembered it myself.

"The vessel's name is *Kathlee,* he spelled the name slowly. The owner's name is one C. Flynn, just as you said."

She withheld a whoop of delight, "Is there a location or address for this Flynn person?"

"No, Captain."

"What is the vessel's location, please?"

The Harbor Master referred to more papers or a notepad. "Oddly enough, the vessel is in our custody at anchorage here. The registered master, this C. Flynn, left suddenly in another, smaller vessel, asking us to keep the *Kathlee* until his return to Port Blair."

"You have been very helpful, sir. The *Bangor* is steaming to your location. I'd like to examine that vessel in your custody and personally thank you for your efforts and ready information on the behalf of my father, owner of *Seatrans*."

"Of course, I recognized your name, Captain," the Harbor Master chuckled. "We look forward to seeing you. *Kathlee's* a strange name for a vessel, don't you think?"

Still elated, she asked, "Why?"

"Well… Most vessel names are longer and masculine, like an animal or a fish."

She giggled. "Well, I think it's perfect! See you soon!"

"Gail, get me the operations officer on this line," he growled.

Out of long practice, his secretary set down her tea cup without spilling a drop.

"Yes, sir!"

She dialed the operations desk on a second line which Mr. Sigmund could not hear.

"Mr Montgomery, the boss is calling. Shall I connect you now?"

"What's his mood?"

"Terrible."

"Thanks. Okay, put me through."

"This is Montgomery in Operations, Mr. Sigmund. What may I do for you, sir?"

"Look at your map. Tell me where is that tanker my daughter captains."

Montgomery activated his screen for the map of Southeast Asia and the Malay Peninsula. "Here it is, sir. Looks like the *Bangor* is nearing Port Blair."

"Port Blair!" Sigmund was dumbfounded until he remembered where he had secretly dispatched that troublesome Capitan Flynn. "I mean," he reminded himself, "the former captain I fired."

"What's my daughter…er…what's the *Bangor* doing there? She's supposed to be enroute to Banda Aceh, isn't she?"

"She," Montgomery nervously flipped through his keypad entries, "recently announced a change of schedule, sir, due to bad weather."

By now the CEO was infuriated. He yelled, "Who authorized that?"

Montgomery sighed with relief once he spotted the entry. "You did, sir, by keypad entry."

Sigmund fumed silently for a full minute. "Cable her and ask for a full report on why she made this change of schedule. Immediately, hear?

"No… wait. I'll call her myself and straighten out this mess. Mr. Montgomery. I strongly suggest you immediately inform me of any such changes to ships' schedules!"

Captain Kathlee Sigmund was having coffee on the bridge and discussing the day's operations with her new First Mate. "Our crew is performing very well, probably because of your hands-on training and supervision. The deck crew connected the output hoses without a hitch this morning. Maybe they've earned some shore leave. What do you think, First Mate?"

"Maybe later, Captain, at a larger port."

"I'm going ashore here to see the Harbor Master and leaving the unloading in your capable hands. Probably be gone a couple of hours."

The First Mate grinned. "What if your father calls again, Captain?"

She finished her coffee and lit a cigarette. "Tell him I'm liaising with the Harbor Master. Tell him about the crew's progress under your supervision and that new maintenance initiative of yours. I'll return his call as soon as I can," she winked an eye.

Nodding, the First Mate said, "We'll be ready to cast off whenever you like, Captain."

Kathlee took a taxi to the Harbor Master's office at port headquarters, anxious to inspect the small skipjack Casey had left behind.

After introducing herself to the Harbor Master, she asked him to repeat his conversation with Casey Flynn.

"Any idea, sir, where Flynn was headed?"

The Harbor Master scratched his beard. "All he said, Captain, was that he was aiming to explore the Andamans and Nicobars."

"That's quite a large area. Did he have a larger vessel than the skipjack he left here?"

"Yes, ma'm. He sailed out of here in a bright yellow yawl with main mast and a single jib. Where he obtained it, I don't know. Wasn't from around here or I would have recognized it."

"Thanks for that information. May I inspect his skipjack now? If he never returns for it, I will reclaim it for *Seatrans*. Have you removed anything from it?"

"Not a thing has been touched aboard it, Captain. It was shipshape when he turned it over to us. We've not bothered to go aboard or even spray the deck.

"Nathaniel here will row you out to it and standby until you're finished."

"Thank you. You've been very helpful and I'll advise *Seatrans* of your help and cooperation. Port Blair is one of our favorites."

Later, back with the Harbor Master, she returned him the skipjack keys with thanks.

"Find any clue to where he went, Captain?"

She shook her head. "No, but I'm very encouraged by what I **didn't** find," she grinned.

She laughed delightedly. "He took the old brass compass I gave him."

"That means," she explained, still ecstatic, "that he's out there somewhere, safe and on course, searching for his Shangri-La. I'll going to look for him where you mentioned-- the Nicobars and Andamans."

"That's a lot of area to search, Captain. Those two chains contain over five hundred islands, although only thirty-seven or so are inhabited."

"Then I'd better start looking for him right away. Goodbye!"

"Good luck, Captain!"

End

ABOUT THE AUTHOR

FORMER REGULAR ARMY and State Department Foreign Service officer Roy Sullivan enjoys Texas history.

In addition to history, he also writes short, one night/one flight mysteries featuring private investigator Jan Kokk from the Caribbean Island of Curacao. The latter is a bon vivant, man-of-the world and sleuth equally at ease with an intriguing mystery or a lovely lady. Kokk, that is, not Sullivan.

Printed in the United States
By Bookmasters